Since retiring as a vice president and treasurer of a Florida-based Fortune 500 company, Jacquel Clark (alias Jay Clark) has instructed thousands of business professionals and authored several articles published in academic journals. This is where she developed her love of writing. As a second career, she now applies her accounting degree and her MBA from Stetson University to provide college students with opportunities to master the skills needed to be successful in future college work and the business world. She teaches accounting and finance-based subjects, and in her spare time, she writes about those things that demand to be put on paper.

Jacquel Clark

THE HIDDEN BURGLAR

AUSTIN MACAULEY PUBLISHERS™

LONDON • CAMBRIDGE • NEW YORK • SHARJAH

Ordering Information
Quantity sales: Special discounts are available on quantity purchases by corporations, associations, and others. For details, contact the publisher at the address below.

Publisher's Cataloging-in-Publication data
Clark, Jacquel
The Hidden Burglar

ISBN 9798886938920 (Paperback)
ISBN 9798889100812 (ePub e-book)

Library of Congress Control Number: 2024902108

www.austinmacauley.com/us

First Published 2024
Austin Macauley Publishers LLC
40 Wall Street, 33rd Floor, Suite 3302
New York, NY 10005
USA

mail-usa@austinmacauley.com
+1 (646) 5125767

Chapter 1

The burglar drew deeply on his cigar and immediately choked with a raspy, throaty cough. He caressed the gray stubble occupying his cheeks and bled the remaining whiskey from his flask. Because he was quiet, unassuming, and a decent football aficionado, Robert Price, or Bobby as most people called him, was likable.

He was a 62-year-old former tradesperson who started community college early but never finished, like so many other things in his life. His actual profession, however, would not sit well with society. Bobby was a burglar-for-hire, and he was quite excellent at it. He enjoyed lifting valuables from the high-brow ingrates in Miami's most affluent and exclusive neighborhoods. He did this for money to avoid getting caught up in inventory management. He didn't target any one group, though; if the price were good, he would steal from anyone.

Parked under an overgrown tree on a stormy night, Bobby waited for the appointed time to enter the mega-house. Every detail of his plan was etched in his mind with a clarity that bordered on obsession—when to enter, where to go, and what to take. He had studied the sketches of the house, mapped out every possible escape route, and memorized every nook and cranny of his route. His contract with his client was clear and concise—he was to steal an envelope containing some papers hidden away on the desk in the first-floor office.

As Bobby sat there, the anticipation building within him, he couldn't help but feel a twinge of excitement. He was stealing paper. No big deal. His profession was boring, but it paid well.

Dark, foreboding clouds were hovering over the horizon, and the night was oppressively humid. The wind roared and howled in all directions, swaying and creaking the old oak trees. Thunder muttered from the blackened sky as the torn leaves from the branches stuck to the windshield. He was sure the thunderstorm would break if he waited until the contracted time, and a torrential downpour would pelt him like bullets, ripping through any cover he might find.

Bobby shifted his gaze to the house, which had about as much personality as a toaster. Nothing more could be said about the home other than the place epitomized all that was disheartening about modern architecture due to its lifelessness and rigid structure. The building evoked thoughts of a prison cell.

Archer Cohen, a long-time friend, had agreed to join him on this trip. Bobby worked alone; however, despite his best efforts, he could not shake the notion that the parameters of this arrangement were not quite right. That, and the impending weather, made him grateful for Archer's presence.

Archer took the title of 'get-away driver', and they both laughed at the silliness of it all, even as Bobby's spine tingled. The clock at last read 10:20. Bobby arrived early and became impatient. He lurched out of the vehicle and stumbled around a bit. At the same time, he tried to cover his head with the hood of his rain jacket, gathered his equipment, which included a waterproof pouch for the plunder, and proceeded to make his way along the side of the house toward the back door.

He yelled to his buddy, "If I'm not back at 10:30, wait longer." Archer grinned as he watched his friend with his lopsided gait disappear into the darkness. He sat in the stillness of the car, watching the anger of the storm, and slipped deep into thought.

An unexpected boom from the back of the house shocked him out of his contemplation. He scoured the area with a wide-eyed glare. The thunder rolled overhead and cried out from the threatening sky. It extended into the night, heralding the arrival of something yet to come.

Now more engaged, Archer was sure he experienced two additional booms with forked lightning, brilliant and white-hot. The vehicle, the residence, and the neighborhood were all encircled by the thunderstorm. The rain quickened, so thick that the monstrous house that had consumed his best friend became invisible.

During this time, Bobby entered the back patio sliding doors and headed to the designated room. The designer went for a minimalist look, with white walls, polished concrete floors, and no chimney. No overflowing piles of clothing, accessories, or toys were visible; only some odd pictures from the family scattered around. This place resembled nothing more than a magazine ad.

After giving the room a critical eye, he walked over to the centerpiece of furniture in the designated room. A loud boom that appeared to originate from the house's second floor rather than the exterior surprised Bobby. He froze and, slowly and steadily, bent down on one knee behind the furniture. His heart rate and respiration increased slightly because he realized the house wasn't unoccupied. Nothing moved, and no sounds from upstairs filtered down to him. Only the rolling thunder outside could be heard. He shook his head and chastised himself for overreacting.

Before he stood, two more booms echoed from the top of the steps. The impression left was that he could reach up and touch them. At first, he thought they were thunderbolts, but the timing was slightly off from the sounds outside the window. Bobby stayed hunkered down and hidden.

Struggling to concentrate, he cast a fleeting glance at his watch. Despite being keenly aware of his early arrival, he mustered the resolve to reach up and swiftly seize the unaddressed manila envelope he had ventured into the house to obtain. The burglar held the goods to his chest, steadying himself. Every muscle in his body alerted him to the impending danger, and he wanted to go.

A few minutes later, after depositing his haul in his waterproof sack and standing up to avoid problems, he found his footing and moved to the door of the room with the desk. He tiptoed toward the back of the house, listening and watching for movement.

To leave without being detected, Bobby had to turn right once outside of the office and go down a long hall to the back patio doors through which he had initially entered. He would pass the staircase, the kitchen on the right, the formal area, and the family room on the left. Behind him would be the entrance door to the house.

The stairs had him worried. Like the rest of the structure, the steps were an attempt at modernity, despite their worn and scuffed appearance. While passing the breakfast nook, the stairwell groaned and creaked as a pair of incalculable feet came pounding down.

Bobby slipped into the galley, trying to control his breathing. His heart raced, and he thought his breathing would announce his presence. He squatted for what must have been an eternity but was minutes. He spent his time hiding, wondering if his mind was playing tricks on him or if this was happening.

He had pulled off hundreds of jobs; why was he spooked now? He peeked around the corner and caught sight of a figure dressed in dark clothing with a knee-length raincoat, and the collar turned up at the neck, moving down the hall. The silhouette swung its head to inspect the formal room, then proceeded to the office. The shape returned, opened the front door, and hesitated a moment. The shadow exited through the door, holding a semi-long, straight object resembling an umbrella in one hand and a small bag in the other.

Bobby waited until he was confident the outline had disappeared before heading for the patio doors. He had started moving toward his goal when he abruptly stopped, turned around, and looked toward the stairway. He needed to understand what, if anything, went on upstairs. His feet would not let him move another step closer to safety.

The burglar paused at the top of the stairs and turned toward the primary bedroom. In front of him, sprawled on the cold cement floor with her limbs and body in complete disarray, was a lifeless middle-aged woman. She was in a pool of fresh blood; her golden-brown hair lay spread about and was covered in sticky red ooze. She had not changed out of her daytime attire: a yellow-orange dress with matching capris. The spot where Bobby stood became unbearably stuffy and stiflingly hot. Significant drops of perspiration formed on his forehead, and he turned and ran in the opposite direction.

He came to a door and glanced in the room without stopping; however, he tripped over his traitorous feet when they stopped on their own and threw him into the door jamb. He looked over hesitantly and became aware of her slumped body, partially sitting and half lying on the unforgiving floor under the room's solitary window.

Not being of legal age, she had her arms wrapped protectively around a young preteen boy whose head was buried deep into her chest. The thief could not see much of her because of the absence of most of her head, which had been replaced with a crimson river that trickled down on her footed pajamas and her brother's head. The youngster had a massive gaping wound in his back. The thief, however, found the stench to be the most unsettling. It was the putrid stink of bowels being released.

Slipping on his stomach's purge, Bobby fell down the steps in his enthusiastic efforts to leave the house of horrors. He went straight out the front door, through the downpour, and headed across the lawn to the vehicle. Smack in the center of the yard, something large yet soft tripped him up and sent his body tumbling face-first into the water-filled grass.

Streaks of pure white zigzagged in the stormy sky and snaked through the air, staying brighter than the midday sun. The burglar recognized the moaning and movement of the impeding object and went to render help.

"Archer, what are you doing out here?" Bobby asked while helping his friend to a sitting position. The older man reached up and touched the back of his head gingerly. His dizziness led to the perception of spinning in a circle, and, without surprise, nausea outpaced all other symptoms, causing him to vomit directly toward Bobby. He jumped back to avoid the catastrophe.

"Nasty headache. Where am I?" the sopping-wet old man replied with slow, slurred words.

"Come on; we have to bounce! This is not good; it's really bad. Help me put you in the car." He struggled to lift his friend. This made him think of a sack of potatoes with no balance, heavy and sloppy.

The howling of sirens in the distance reminded Bobby of doleful electric screams. As he listened, fear started to curl up inside. It clung to his ribs and settled uncomfortably into his chest. He knew the reaction would stay, reminding him of its existence every time he opened his mouth to breathe. Bobby's mind began to fail; he had trouble formulating a thought. Dead. All three of them were murdered! Mired in the sludge-like quicksand and every movement impossible, he could not figure a way out.

While concentrating on shoving Archer into the automobile, the burglar's teeth chattered in an intrusive manner due to his quivering jaw. After finishing the chore, he tightened the framework around his teeth and took a long breath to regain control. This caused him to clue in again on the siren but this time it was much closer. The sound poured gasoline on the spark of fear now in his belly.

Bobby jumped into the driver's seat of the sedan, the key still in the ignition, and with the speed of a Hellcat, the mega-house soon became a memory. Upon leaving the neighborhood, his instincts guided him to make a left turn just as two police cars zoomed past, deftly deactivating their sirens and extinguishing their lights. Bobby glanced at the clock on the dashboard, which read 10:40.

Chapter 2

The radio squelched, and the dispatcher's voice emanated through the static, "Please be advised, there's a 10-64 with shots fired at 1620 Angel Bluff Road. 10-85, I repeat, 10-85." Rita Slater and her partner were out of service for lunch but quickly responded that they were on their way.

They flipped on their sirens and lights until they approached the subdivision given by the dispatcher. They went in silent as instructed. Another cruiser joined, and the four officers rolled up to the location in eerie silence.

The precipitation had slowed in its fury, but the heavens were still throwing thunderclaps and lightning bolts. Despite the unsettling truth that danger was waiting, the cops surveyed the home and concentrated on the open front door. One patrolman went down the right side of the house, one down the left, and two approached from the front. Secondary locations were cleared and radioed to front-facing teams, allowing them to breach a normally inaccessible residence.

When the first official walked up the steps, he saw the corpse lying face down in the entryway to the bedroom on the right. She appeared to be crawling. The second lawman turned to the left to clear the rest of the second floor. He investigated the first open door, immediately turned, hurried down the stairs, avoiding the vomit at the top of the stairway, and ran to the yard to purge his recent meal. By this time, another cruiser had joined the effort.

After confirming that first aid was unnecessary, the most senior person at the murder location, Rita, contacted the medical examiner, the watch commander, and the others on her contact list; she established the dwelling as a crime scene and secured the perimeter. Outdoor illumination was erected to supplement the ineffective streetlights and fight the moonless sky's darkness. The generator roared loud and obnoxiously.

After hearing a dispatcher order him to go to the hospital, Dave Mansfield could barely understand the rest of what the messenger was saying. It seemed there had been a collision. The helicopter overhead sped him from the current crime scene toward the hospital. The faster he wanted to go, the darker it became, and the slower he went. He needed help. Why didn't anyone bring help? He was getting weaker by the second.

He found himself alone in the pitch black, hearing a voice inform him they had died. The voice was his enemy, and he struggled against it. Alarms went off, but he struggled against them also. They sounded again, and Mansfield jerked awake.

He reached over to pick up his phone, and it sat silent. He wondered exactly how many rings he had missed. He checked the caller ID before putting the phone on the table.

He looked around absentmindedly and realized he had fallen asleep while working on the jigsaw puzzle sprawled before him on the kitchen table. Mansfield enjoyed puzzles. It gave him a quiet, solo break from his job's bustle and unrelenting stimulus. He rubbed his eyes and face, picked up a piece, and added it to the puzzle. A slight smile crossed his lips as he congratulated himself.

He stood up and stretched out the kinks, took a couple of Tylenol out of the cabinet, and washed them down with the remnants of some left-over whiskey. Even though he couldn't see anything but darkness outside, his ears could still pick up the sound of a strong wind sweeping down the beach. The clock on the wall indicated it wasn't even time for the 11:00 news.

Mansfield resided in the South of Fifth area in Miami Beach. He couldn't afford the property, yet he was there, nonetheless. He bought the house with the insurance money he received after the deaths of his wife and son many years ago. He walked onto his balcony and smelled the Atlantic Ocean on the wild wind that caused the rain to fall horizontally. Back inside, the kitchen table was littered with a bottle of Jack Daniels and a half-empty package of cigarettes. He found the phone and returned the call.

"Izzy, what have you got for me?" Mansfield asked once he was transferred to the commander on duty. His real name was Everett Izquierdo, but everyone called him Izzy.

"Yep, you got a three-for-one, Mansfield. I know you just finished a case, but you're still scheduled to work until the late shift tomorrow night. Both you and your buddy. So that means you get the DBs in Angel Bluff."

"What else?"

"Patrol has already checked it out. Medical Examiner is on the way."

"How did we get the call?"

"Anonymous to 911. The dispatcher said it came at 10:35 from a pay phone. Wouldn't leave a name. Anything else?" Izzy asked.

"Yes, tell your guys not to mess with my site, and call Landers and tell him to meet me. I'm on my way."

Mansfield changed clothes, brushed his teeth very carefully because he had been having a molar problem, and grabbed a couple of packs of cigarettes from the cabinet where he stored his overstock. He had never smoked until he moved to Miami. In final preparation, he opened the locked safe and took out his holster and his Glock 22, the gun that now served as his service weapon. This was a recent change for the department.

Previously, for many years, Mansfield used a Glock Model 17 mm. His backup was the tried-and-true Smith & Wesson 38 Special. On many past occasions, this firearm had saved his life. Recently, he had added a semi-automatic assault rifle to his arsenal.

Securely stored in his trunk, he now possessed an AR-15. Just a few weeks earlier, owning, let alone carrying, this formidable weapon would have been illegal for him. However, with the expiration of the Federal Assault Weapon Ban enacted by President Clinton in 1994 and no replacement in sight, law enforcement now faced criminals armed with comparable firepower. The menacing presence of this weapon in Mansfield's possession symbolized his endeavor to level the playing field.

On his way out, he glanced in the mirror and pulled his fingers through his shoulder-length, thick, once completely blonde curly hair. Now, the curls were interspersed with gray. He paused and studied the wrinkles forming around his 45-year-old cobalt blue eyes and the blonde stubble on his chin. At least it covered the one small scar he had earned in a motorcycle accident 10 years ago.

He did not bother shaving because his clients would not care. He got into his department-issued sedan and took the MacArthur Causeway to I-95 South. After a jig and a jag, 25 minutes later, he drove into the Angel Bluff neighborhood. Landers had already arrived.

Detective Mansfield and his partner, Mike Landers, arrived to find an investigative team deep into their work. Both detectives paused and observed the area, noting everything possible before entering the site. Reporters gathered in the street like black vultures, signaling that the dead were in the vicinity. These reporters were not picky, they digested most anything that didn't have a pulse, and if given a choice, they always went for the fresh kill.

Photographers, collection experts, and the coroner were circling about. Detective Mansfield pondered the coordinated efforts as though composing modern classical music. However, he was aware that no crime scene, no piece of evidence, and no investigative strategy were ever the same.

Mansfield glanced over at Landers as a cigarette dangled from his lips and mumbled, "These composers might orchestrate their music tonight, my friend." Then, looking up at the sky, he pulled his slicker tighter around his chest and walked toward the nightmare awaiting him. Damn, his tooth hurt! He wanted to spit out his teeth like stones. Landers stood for a minute, wondering what in the hell his partner was talking about.

Mansfield found the busy Rita Slater. He crushed the cigarette butt on the sidewalk and picked it up to dispose of it properly. Rita seemed young, but then everyone was young to him these days. She was in her thirties. Her black hair was pulled back in a bun so tight that her facial skin stretched, leaving the impression of a caricature. She walked professionally, she was aware of the protocol, and her work was all-consuming. She had lost her identity in her career.

Mansfield's face and hair were dripping wet. He fished around until he produced a hair tie big enough for the weight of his hair and to pull the massive bulk of curls away from his face. This succeeded in accentuating his chiseled jawline. In his experience, most females found a strong jawline physically pleasing and a sign of strength and dominance.

Like every other woman Dave Mansfield encountered, Slater hesitated when she saw him. Her mouth opened slightly, and it was over as quickly as it happened. Slater took both detectives on a preliminary walk-through.

"The suspect entered through the patio sliding door and exited through the front door—no living witnesses in the house. The residence belongs to Mr. Mark and Evie Moody. They have lived here for 15 years and have two children—Victoria, aged 16, and Cooper, aged 11." Rita took a minute to regroup her thoughts as they arrived at the foot of the stairs.

"Up the stairs, to the right, is one primary crime scene containing Evie Moody. She died of a shotgun wound directly to the upper chest cavity. Down the hall to the left, the second primary has both children. Victoria died of a shotgun wound directly to the head, and the boy was hit directly in the core of his back. No shells have been recovered." Rita paused and waited for questions from the detectives.

"Where is the father?" Landers asked.

"Unknown currently. We are trying to locate him."

"Has anyone canvassed the neighborhood for potential witnesses? If not, can we get that started immediately? Most of them are standing in the street waiting to be fed," Mansfield directed. He was angry, angry at the waste, angry at the rainstorm, and most of all, angry at the pain in his tooth.

"Why do you think the perp went to the back of the house?" asked Mansfield.

"Because the door seemed to be unlocked. It was also wiped clean for prints," Slater responded. Since the technicians were still attending to the bodies, Mansfield and Landers started their search of the house outside the back patio door.

Looking around, Landers commented, "He got into the house before the downpour. No water tracks of any kind here, and everything is washed clean outside. What was that, about 10:00, a little after?" Mansfield replied with a grunt, looking elsewhere in the family room. He walked to the kitchen and sized it up—nothing unusual.

"His business was not in either of these rooms. The suspect or suspects were familiar with the house or had been given specific instructions on where to go once in," declared Mansfield. To help him focus, his old habit of chewing on a toothpick usually came in handy, but that wasn't happening tonight. Just speaking sent a sharp and throbbing pain down the length of his body.

Following the perp's suspected route, Mansfield walked down the hall toward the front door and paused at the stairwell. Before going up, he continued a little further and walked into the formalized living area where the baby grand piano made its statement.

"Interesting," commented Landers as he followed Mansfield into the room. Landers referred to his notepad and made a note to find out who played. There was nothing amiss in this space, either. Only fresh-turned carpet fibers were visible after a thorough vacuuming, leaving no trace of footsteps.

Across the hall was an office. Everything was in order, but Mansfield hesitated. The only desk in the room was situated centrally, and bookcases lined three of the four walls. The bookshelves mostly contained collectible beer steins sorted by country and year. Hundreds of antiques occupied the shelves.

Mansfield wasn't sure what was bothering him, so he asked Landers to photograph each piece of each wall for him to review later. The drawers on the desk were locked. After a technician unlocked the desk, the detectives rifled through the contents and asked the investigative team to pack everything.

Halfway up the stairs, the smell of death permeated the atmosphere. Each detective put on their mask to help with the stench. Stepping around the woman sprawled in the bedroom doorway, Landers entered the room where the parents slept.

As with the rest of the house, few items indicated personal choice or preference. The room was as bland and generic as the rest of the house. The jewelry box stood on its own next to the dresser. Fingerprints were being taken although it didn't appear anyone had touched it or its contents.

Looking into the closet, Landers mainly found women's clothing, with only a few items belonging to a man. He smiled, thinking that is how it is in most marriages. The bathroom did not render surprises either. As far as he was concerned, this room could have been plucked off any movie set and dropped in this house.

Meanwhile, Mansfield turned left at the head of the stairs toward the children's bedrooms. The first room was Cooper's. This room was lived in and was the focal point of this child's world. The lone window in the room was adjacent to a twin-sized bed. Cooper was an active boy, as seen by his choice of playthings—a baseball bat, a soccer ball, and a skateboard, all of which quickly met Mansfield's eye.

A few feet from Mansfield, the boy's sister fought to keep him safe. She cradled him tightly and shielded him from the door and everything that might come through it. On the wall was a pinboard with pictures of Cooper and his friends in various degrees of fun. He had many sports photos pinned up and some academic ribbons from school displayed. The bed was crumpled where he had been sleeping, or had it remained unmade from the previous night?

Landers appeared as Mansfield was leaving the room to inspect the final bedroom, a standard room for a teenager. It had an unmistakable vibe of youthful exuberance and personal expression. The walls were adorned with an eclectic mix of posters featuring the current pop stars Britney Spears, NSYNC, and Avril Lavigne. Against one wall stood a desk adorned with a clutter of books, colorful notepads, and neon gel pens.

Her closet was full of a variety of fashion choices. The more accessible racks of clothing featured goth-like colors and styles. A collection of chunky plastic accessories, brightly colored beaded necklaces, jelly bracelets, and oversized hoop earrings were displayed on a pegboard. In contrast to the rest of the house, this room and Cooper's room were typical.

It seemed as if Victoria had suddenly stood up, knocked over the soft stool at the make-up vanity, and then left the room. Her make-up case was open, and the brushes were lying about. Her cell phone was lying on the ground, close to the stool. Mansfield noticed the bed was appropriately dressed, and the nightstand featured a picture of Victoria with an older male standing arm-in-arm. He walked over and marked the picture so it would be gathered as evidence.

Landers picked up her cell phone and noted that she must have been texting during the break-in. He wrote down the number and name saved on the phone and tagged it for evidence, along with the computer occupying her double-sized bed.

Chapter 3

Dave Mansfield made it to his Wednesday morning appointment with Dr. Alex Williams, DDS., despite it being an early hour. The relentless agony had plagued him for the past three days, originating from the previous Saturday night while he played poker with his friends.

During that moment, when he indulged in a sip of his whiskey on the rocks, the suction caused by swallowing triggered an unsettling sensation as if his back tooth had been drained dry. The onslaught of excruciating pain coursed through the tooth's length, penetrating deep into his jaw. Unfortunately, the timing couldn't have been worse, as it was the weekend, and no dental clinics were available until Monday.

Mansfield carefully evaluated the pros and cons of seeking emergency room assistance, ultimately opting to alleviate his suffering using a stash of hydrocodone he had saved from a prior injury. Since his regular dentist couldn't accommodate him until Wednesday, he resigned himself to endure the torment, inducing self-imposed sedation as he patiently waited for relief. After surviving a couple of the most agonizing days of the decade, he finally found solace in the knowledge that someone would soon be able to end this wretched pain.

After X-rays, Alex explained, "Well, Dave, your rear molar has a severe cavity. Given its depth, it appears unlikely I can salvage it without resorting to a root canal procedure. Today, I'm going to excavate the decay from the tooth. However, if the decay has extensively progressed, we may have to consider extracting the entire tooth."

"I don't care. Just make the damn thing stop pounding. My current case needs my full attention, and I can hardly think with this tooth throbbing every second of every day. This can't go on any longer!"

The dentist advised, "All right, you may feel a slight sting here, but there's nothing to be concerned about," the dentist reassured, gently inserting the needle along the gum line while giving the jaw a subtle wiggle. Mansfield teetered on the edge of flight, his mind filled with mundane thoughts as if an insatiable worm was voraciously devouring his face from within. This peculiar mental image only intensified his dental apprehension, but eventually, he calmed himself down.

He thanked Alex enthusiastically when his tooth was extracted amid the buzzing and grinding of electric equipment. Although gauze was still in his mouth, he did not experience any discomfort. Dr. Williams reminded him of appropriate oral hygiene and warned him of some soreness, but not as much as he had previously experienced. Mansfield accepted the pain medicine, which he was sure he would not need, left the dental office, and headed for the squad room.

The detective walked through the back door, past the drunk tank, and took the rear stairs to the homicide bureau. This was a regular day, with phones ringing and people moving around. Landers filed the Investigating Officer's Chronological Record form into the Murder Book. This was the case file structure used by Miami Homicide to organize and standardize their case files.

The Moody Murder Book consisted of all case-related materials outlined in specific sections. The detective responsible for maintaining the Murder Book had to be careful and competent, as the book was discoverable. Landers always accepted this responsibility.

"What do you have so far? My memory from last night is a bit fuzzy," Mansfield said through one side of his mouth as he sat at his desk across from Landers.

"Not much. I slept a few hours in the bunk and then chased Mr. Moody down. He is a renowned concert pianist. Honestly, this is incredible. He performs solo recitals and concertos, in which he joins an orchestra, as well as competitions and corporate events. Every performance, he gets at least $75,000, plus the cost of travel and lodging," Landers answered, shaking his head in disbelief.

However, when Mansfield attempted to blow a whistle, all that was heard and seen was spit and blood. Leaning over the trash can, he removed the old gauze and replaced it with the new one the dentist had given him.

"Nice." Landers laughed. "How did the dentist go anyway?"

"He took the tooth out. Despite my improvement, Novocain continues to be effective. Well, we know who plays the piano in the house. So is the guy on tour now or what?"

"Yes. He's on an Austrian tour and is currently in Salzburg. We notified the person representing him, and he will pass along a message for Mr. Moody to contact us immediately. No word from him yet, probably due to the time difference."

"Okay, so we have Mom and the two kids killed by someone with a shotgun while Dad is out of the country. Patrol rolled on a robbery in progress with shots fired. Didn't the coroner say the bodies were dead less than an hour by the time they arrived? Do we know how the dispatcher got the information? Who arrived first, and how long?" Mansfield asked as he leaned back in his chair and started to put the first pieces of the timeline together. He seemed much more himself than he had been the night before.

Landers pulled up the 911 call log and discovered the call came from an unidentified caller at 10:35 pm on Tuesday, October 19, 2004. He could not tell if the caller was male or female. The 911 operator dispatched a patrol at 10:37. Switching to the dispatcher tapes, Landers told Mansfield that two cars arrived at the scene at 10:42 and a third car at 10:44. By 10:50, the house and its surroundings had been cleared.

"The crime scene log-in sheets indicated the coroner arrived at 11:15 pm. He mentioned that the corpses were still warm. That leaves the perp on scene anywhere close to 10:15 to 10:42, 20 minutes before the 911 call and about seven minutes after," Landers summarized.

"Okay, that's excellent news. Do we have the notes from the canvas of the neighbors regarding what they may have witnessed that we can check? I will work through those while you continue with the background on each family member." Mansfield reached over into the pile of papers on Landers' desk and found the interview sheets.

Customers at the Bat Cave could enjoy their drinks in peace. The thug behind the bar with the nicotine-stained teeth and grouchy attitude determined who stayed and who was a two-minute observer. You would know you were accepted if a bowl of stale pretzels or peanuts magically appeared before you. To protect the privacy of its customers, the pub only took cash.

The long-mirrored bar contained hundreds of alcohol bottles, but Mansfield always ordered his usual whiskey on the rocks. He wished he were at the Bat Cave now instead of reading these dreary reports. He glanced at the clock and saw that lunchtime was nearing. He had finally finished reviewing the last sheet in the pile, and his stomach growled.

"Hey, Landers, how you doing over there? Hungry?" Dave asked.

"Doing good. Great stuff here. I'm always hungry. How's your mouth? Are you going to be able to eat?" Mike peered up from his computer screen and grinned.

"A bit tender, but I think I can manage." The two detectives grabbed their notes and headed down the stairs.

Chapter 4

Bobby pulled over 15 minutes down the road to see how Archer was doing. He'd been attempting to communicate with him since they left the mega-house, but Archer stopped speaking and slumped down in the seat. Bobby shook him to wake him up. Nothing. He shook him more firmly and spoke more loudly. Archer finally moved.

"Where am I?" He struggled to sit up. "What happened?" Archer's speech still appeared slurred and slow.

"Remember, you are the get-away driver," Bobby encouraged. "Only you got out of the car for some reason and got clobbered on the head. Did a branch hit you, or did someone attack you?" Archer's fingertips brushed the back of his head, and he was covered in blood.

"Where am I? What happened?" Archer repeated, looking at his hand and laying his head against the window.

Bobby had a rudimentary understanding of concussions, but the little he did possess informed him that he needed to have Archer checked out by a medical professional. He turned around and headed straight for Mercy Hospital.

Once at the emergency room, many people rushed to help Archer out of the vehicle and lift him onto a stretcher. A nurse asked him where he hurt, and he gestured to the right side of the back of his head. Despite his limited ability to articulate, Archer somehow managed to convey to her the sensation of his skull relentlessly pounding against his flesh. He described it as the most excruciating headache he had ever endured. The doctors administered fentanyl to lessen his pain. Although it didn't completely alleviate the headache, it did succeed in significantly diminishing his level of concern.

After completing the CT scan and the stitching procedure, Archer stayed at the hospital for observation. The doctor concluded that a blunt object striking the head from behind caused a concussion. There was no sign of tree shrapnel in the immediate area of the injury. Archer was expected to recover fully, as he sustained no internal injuries. After a week of rest and no physical endeavors, he could return to normal activities after the wound had healed.

Bobby was famished and pulled in at a Dunkin' Donuts on the way home. Two glazed and a vanilla creme filled with a large coffee, complete with cream, and two Splendas later, he drew calm, smooth breaths. Sugar was the last thing he needed, but it sure tasted right. His thoughts raced through the night's events, seeking order or sense in the chaos.

In his mind, the thoughts sped about like a train without plans to stop. In the distance, he saw the taillights of each unrelated occurrence fade away. He pondered which idea would be the clue that would anchor the overall structure of this conundrum.

He arrived home just as the sun barely touched the horizon, bringing with it the promise of a day filled with warmth and light. Bobby scurried down the path toward his house, his damp shoes slapping against the stone steps that led to the front door. Fallen leaves and storm debris littered the walkway, bathing it in dark colors, twigs, and small branches.

The porch light had that familiar radiance that made the house feel welcoming and comfortable. He easily turned the doorknob, and the metal felt refreshing against his palm as he did so. He then stepped into the dimly lit living room.

The house had been through a rough patch in its history. Years ago, the paint on the walls was smooth, and white window frames stood out in a sea of blue. After seasons with no thought to maintenance, the location had been reduced to the kind of place realtors hate to list.

The interior's outdated fixtures, many of which had become rusted and stained, drastically lowered the property's value. For Bobby, it was perfect. As a turtle retreats into its shell, so does Bobby upon returning home. After a troubled night, he found safety in this dwelling, his resting place.

When Bobby finished setting his equipment and the file on the kitchen table, he walked straight to the bathroom, showered, and changed into clean, dry clothing. Six hours later, he woke up and groggily looked around. In the same position where he had sat on the bed and leaned back for a minute to relax, he found every blasted muscle in his body ached when he moved. He made it to the recliner in the living room, where he sat down and turned on the television.

The news had a special report titled 'Mom and Kids Slain in Angel Bluff—Where's Daddy?' The news report went over everything Bobby already knew. However, the bombshell was that a neighbor reported a strange car parked between the big house and the house next door for around 30 minutes before the police arrived. Because of the weather, the witness could not tell if the vehicle was occupied. The news reporter described Bobby's car but, thankfully, did not have the plate numbers.

It took Bobby some time to process the news report before he moved. Incredulity was palpable, as was his pessimistic outlook, and he arched his brows in surprise. Bobby's lean frame slumped like a two-decade hobo on a wooden park bench, every splinter making its presence known. He rubbed his face and three-day stubble, trying to escape this nightmare.

Instead, he only thought about the police looking through every email and file. In just a few short days, they would discover the evidence, the breadcrumbs, which would bring them directly back to him. Bobby envisioned the orange jumpsuit with his name stenciled on the back. His heart ached, and his brain was full of useless mush. There were ways out, but was he tough enough to step in that direction?

Chapter 5

A young woman delivered a child in 1969, and she wept. He was one more lost soul to add to the Decretei, those born after Decree 770 in Romania. Decree 770 was a communist decree limiting abortion and contraception. Nicolae Ceausescu, the communist leader at the time, envisioned creating a larger Romanian population to fuel industrialization.

While growing up in rural Romania, Yetta's coffee of choice consisted of musty barns, mildew, and fertilizers. Deep furrows of dark earth churned up during the plowing season reminded her of newly turned graves. Mostly, she had nothing more than her dirty hands, grit under her fingernails, and sweat-stiff clothes to wear. In the early 1960s, modernization and industrialization prompted her relocation to urban centers. She hoped this would lead to a better standard of living, one above poverty.

A rapidly growing middle class caused housing shortages. Countless apartment structures materialized and were immediately inhabited despite having no running water or heating. Yetta woke to the sounds of people chatting and yelling, the whir of bicycle tires, and the slapping of shoes on cobblestones instead of the worn-out rooster of her childhood. Her first deep breaths consisted of old cigarette smoke, urine, sewage, and old water in rain puddles. She'd exchanged one insignificant life for another.

Disgusted by the news of the passage of Decree 770, Yetta became fully aware that with children, she would not be able to support herself. As a matter of patriotic duty, Decree 770 required all Romanian women under 45 to bear at least five children. Political leaders instantly set up a robust system of control to enforce this decree. She needed to act quickly.

Additionally, she was required to have gynecological examinations every month as part of her government-funded medical care and other services. Privy to terrifying accounts of pregnancies discovered by government officials and tracked until delivery, Yetta became more scared than disgusted. Friends who tried to provoke termination paid for their attempts with years in prison, where cold metal bars and pitted concrete walls became their homes.

Yetta reasoned that her healthiest path would be abstaining from sexual activity. She put in long hours at work, put money aside, and made plans to leave Romania. This worked until the organization of the Demographic Committees. These committees supervised pregnancy tests to be performed at the factories every three months.

With these changes, every unmarried adult over 25 experienced a 10% increase in their tax bill. Both partners experienced an even higher rate of increase if they hadn't given birth after two years of marriage with no medical rationale.

She finally decided to do something about this. Yetta set up surveillance after occasionally seeing fliers critical of Decree 770 being circulated. She was sure the pretense of patriotism should not fall upon the women in a country's society. A bottomless pit swallowed her emotions, leaving her with nothing. Everything that might go wrong, had! Any person with such anti-state propaganda would face the wrath of the state's highest authorities, but she was beyond that.

She found a spot near a plant and lurked there every night, waiting for someone to come by and put up a bulletin. While the wind howled like a pack of Arctic wolves, she crouched under her newspaper and bits of blanket. Yetta barely felt it. The bricks at her back from the occupants on the other side warmed her up a little.

Wild cats howling in the distance became audible despite the intense winds. With a smile, she pulled her rough cap below her eyebrows and burrowed into her warm corner next to the dumpster. The mission gave her hope.

In the second week, a dark-brown form appeared, tall and imposing. He was hardly visible due to the thick fog and the consequent obscurity. He evaporated as soon as Yetta blinked her eyes. She exited from her den and set out to find him. To her disappointment, he was still gone as she stood motionless in the cobbled alley. She walked up to read the posted material when a sonorous voice startled her.

"Why are you stalking me?" Ekon, a West African who attended the University of Bucharest, asked. He was a staunch opponent of Ceausescu and worked conscientiously to undermine the party. Ekon had a passion for writing, painting, and secretly distributing posters. He worked in the shadows in unique ways.

Yetta was furious with herself for letting someone creep so close to her without noticing. Calmly, she replied, "What makes you think I am stalking you?"

"Because you are here, and so am I," Ekon answered.

"When the scratching of your shoes woke me up, I realized you pinned this note. I couldn't help but be interested, so I got up to check out what you put on the pole."

"First, I did not put anything on this foul pole. Second, there is no moonlight. You would not be able to read a thing," Ekon challenged.

Yetta argued, "Do you see anyone else around? That leaves you as the one who made the posting."

"Are you falsely accusing me of a crime?" Ekon's tone shifted.

"Uh, no. I guess I thought you put something up. Since you most likely walked up to read the note, I may have misinterpreted your actions." Yetta said, apprehensive and a little afraid.

"To reiterate, if it is too dark for you to read, it is too dark for me. Exactly who are you, and why are you watching me?" Ekon moved in a little closer.

"Listen, you are about to make me angry. Step off. I only want to be part of whatever you have going on. Who are you?" Yetta had to squint to see the man due to his dark skin and opaque garments. She was only able to discern his eyes.

Ekon bet she would have liked to have had his name. After warning her to mind her business, Ekon disappeared for the second time that night. Yetta thought joining the group would be easier. After introspection, she concluded that she would behave similarly if involved in criminal activity.

Over the next few months, Yetta knew she was being watched and monitored more closely than usual. Neither the police nor the mysterious Black man from the wee hours could be identified. She continued picking out spots for posting propaganda and waited for someone to show up.

The Black man eventually approached her about a private gathering. At the meeting, she met others who, like her, wanted Romania to part with its communist past. Growing more aware of the inequities in society and how some are targeted, she worked with others to bring about change. In addition to Ceausescu, prejudice and racism ran rampant in Romania. The country barely had a handful of Africans, and the government did not treat them with dignity.

The revolutionary group was detected within the year. Everyone except Yetta disappeared after being apprehended. She was temporarily spared because of her pregnancy. Doctors from the government kept an eye on her until she produced a healthy Black child. Upon Yetta's execution, the infant was deposited in an orphanage run by the state.

Healthy children stayed at the orphanage until age six. After that, students found their way to establishments managed by the Ministry of Education, where they received some schooling. But those with disabilities, illnesses, or physical differences went to isolated facilities: Homes for the Deficient and Unsalvageable. This was the destination of Yetta's nameless baby boy.

Chapter 6

As a result of Austria's rich musical heritage, Mark Moody's manager, Darryl Jenkins, arranged a four-stop tour in the country. The trip began at Innsbruck, the city that hosted the Winter Olympics twice. This city had so much to offer guests that classical concerts were only one of the possibilities offered. Therefore, modest to medium-sized engagements were the rule rather than the exception.

Small commitments annoyed Mark. To save him time, he repeatedly advised Darryl about booking these encounters. It took the same amount of time and effort to ensure the piano provided worked properly and to create a suitable presentation for these venues as it did for the larger ones. Because the benefit never outweighed the expense, his time was consistently squandered. Mark bolted after the Innsbruck show, which drew about 150 concertgoers, to avoid a brawl with the paying customers.

"Darryl, where on earth did these Neanderthals come from?" Mark snapped.

"They're only the people from the town who bought tickets. Why? What's wrong?"

"Are you kidding? Latecomers barged in unceremoniously, causing disruptions among the seated guests and creating a chaotic commotion. The sporadic clapping that accompanied specific gestures and musical elements only heightened the distressing atmosphere. The whole experience shook me to the depths of my being, leaving me profoundly unsettled."

Mark's intense focus zeroed in on Darryl, his narrowed eyes resembling the slit-like pupils of a pit viper. Observing Mark's piercing gaze, Darryl couldn't help but gulp anxiously. A seething animosity brewed within Darryl's sphere of emotions as he sensed that Mark held him responsible for the disturbance, intensifying their tension.

"I understand; no more small gigs after we leave Austria. Got it," Darryl stuttered.

The next stop on the itinerary was Salzburg, the setting for the 1965 filming of The Sound of Music. The hefty price paid for Mark Moody's booking was evidence of his genius. Salzburg had long been famous for its music festivals, as seen by its many historic theaters and concert halls.

Other major Salzburg festivals included Mozart Week, a weeklong winter event focusing on the work of the great Austrian composer, and Salzburg Cultural Days, an annual two-week festival in October that included symphonic and chamber concerts and opera performances. This festival was why Mark Moody had traveled to Salzburg.

This time around, the show was spectacular for Mark. He was in higher spirits than usual. The Salzburg Music Hall was a captivating architectural masterpiece with soaring ceilings adorned with ornate chandeliers that cast a warm and inviting glow upon the space. The seating area was carefully arranged semi-circularly to ensure every seat offered an unobstructed view of the stage, creating an intimate connection between Mark and his audience. The size and acoustics of the stage were meticulously designed to capture every nuanced sound, which allowed the music to resonate throughout the space with perfect clarity.

No cell phone rang during the event as the audience was well-versed in proper conduct. Mark left the stage after he was done, but he returned for an encore and played a short jazz tune, which delighted the audience.

Mark and his crew ventured out of the hotel and into the city's beer gardens for a modest celebration, knowing that Salzburg was widely recognized as Austria's beer capital. Mark found a spot to relax in the garden on the white limestone that covered the ground of an old Augustinian monastery. All around, chestnut trees stood proud, sharing their shade.

Here, he met some intriguing locals while feasting and relaxing, and they insisted he sign up for the Eagle's Nest in Berchtesgaden Tour before leaving for Vienna. He'd be able to see Hellbrunn Castle before traveling up to the Eagle's Nest, Hitler's former mountain home in Bavaria, on a half-day guided tour. Mark knew he and his crew would head out for Vienna tomorrow morning. But he wanted to go on this tour.

He found Darryl and told him to postpone his reservation until tomorrow night. Everyone else could stick to the plan, but he wanted to leave tomorrow evening. Darryl said that would be fine, but he would move along with the crew.

Pounding on the door disturbed his inebriated stupor. After numerous loud bangs, his eyes opened fully, and he realized he was awake. Stumbling toward the door, he began to mutter incoherently, "Stop, stop the noise. I'm coming. Who's bugging me?" When he looked through the peephole, Mark saw a dreadful-looking Darryl.

"What now? Why are you here at this ridiculous hour? Has someone done something stupid?" Mark asked, yawning and rubbing his eyes. Darryl entered the room and locked the door, grabbing Mark by the arm and directing him to sit down. Mark shook off Darryl's grab and said grumpily, "What is it?"

"Have you talked with your wife or the kids since we left?"

"What?" Mark rubbed his eyes and stared at his manager. "You woke me up to ask me that? No. Unless there's an emergency that she can't manage, I never talk to them until I return. Why are you asking such a foolish question?"

"I… I just got a call from the States, and…"

"Spit it out, man, for Mozart's sake. Do you need to go home for something? Go ahead. I can manage."

"Oh, no. Not me!" Darryl took a step back from Mark. "Burglarized… your house… and…"

"What! The fuckers. What did they take? Why didn't the fuzz contact Evie? I can't do anything from the other side of the world. Where was Evie? The kids? Why are they calling us?" Mark stopped pacing and turned to look straight at Darryl.

"Well, I was trying to tell you, but you interrupted. Mark, please sit down."

"I don't think I want to sit down." Mark's arrogance began to wane, and he gripped the chair's arm for support.

"The detectives are conducting an investigation, and they urgently need you to come home," Darryl relayed, his voice tinged with concern. He moved closer to Mark, witnessing the visible signs of shock as his knees trembled.

"They found three bodies in the house… hey, hold on, let me help you," Darryl said, assisting Mark in finding a seat. After a moment, Mark lifted his gaze toward Darryl, now seemingly fully aware of his surroundings.

"Do you mean to say they're gone? Everyone… they're dead!" Mark's voice trembled with terror, his words echoing through the room. Darryl attempted to calm him, gently urging him to lower his voice.

"What exactly happened?" Mark inquired, his voice filled with confusion and desperation.

"I'm not entirely sure. The policewoman didn't provide me with any details. They passed along a message requesting you to give them a call," Darryl replied, trying to offer some reassurance.

"To hell with that. Can you immediately book my flight back home? We must cancel the remainder of the tour and ensure everyone returns quickly. Once we land, contact the authorities again and inform them. I want someone to meet me," Mark declared; his words rushed as he paced the room, occasionally biting down on the cuticle of his right thumb. Darryl provided solace by assuring him he would handle the situation and return later with the necessary travel arrangements.

After Darryl left his room, Mark paced for a few minutes, then sat down and put his head in his hands. *How is this possible? What does this mean? Charles! Can they find out about Charles?* Mark promptly left his hotel room and walked downstairs to use a phone privately and prevent anyone from overhearing. He dialed the number from memory.

The man answered the phone on the first ring. "Charles, have you heard the news? They have died unexpectedly. I'm in Salzburg, and the officers just got word to Darryl. Are you safe?" Mark spoke frantically.

"I'm fine. Yes, it has been on the news all day as a special report. The report said the police were looking for you. I guess they have not updated it yet. Mark, I'm so sorry?" Charles replied.

"How did they die? Did they suffer?"

"It doesn't sound like it. All three of them died of shotgun wounds. Once I thought about the possible arrival of the cops, I got out of the flat as quickly as possible. At the station now, and I doubt they are aware of me, so they should not come here," Charles said with empathy.

"At least one less thing to worry about. Darryl is booking my trip home as we speak. I will come home as soon as I can. I love you." Mark hung up the phone and returned to his room, full of grief.

Darryl came with the itinerary about 30 minutes later, indicating Mark would arrive in Miami at 7:00 pm US time. Officer Rita Slater would be at the airport to meet him.

Chapter 7

Landers studied his friend while he tried to negotiate eating lunch on just one side of his mouth. On occasion, Mansfield's head would tilt to the right as food attempted to escape to the other side. This was comical and sad to witness. In his heart, Landers was happy he wasn't the one suffering. Three waitresses strolled by a dozen times, checking on Dave, each wanting to sympathize and get to know him better. Mansfield grew irritated, but Landers always succeeded in being entertained by this ritual.

Unlike Dave, Miami investigator Mike Landers was a native son of the city. The story of his thrill at passing the detective's exam and being assigned to the homicide unit, thanks to his excellent grades, became his favorite anecdote. Everyone wanted to buy him a drink to bask in his triumph, so fellow officers flocked to the Skeeter Eater, the local cop bar. Even the seniors attended. His captain didn't hold back his eagerness to share that Mike's new comrade was Dave Mansfield. Everyone enjoyed a hearty chuckle, but the news dampened Mike's enthusiasm.

Even though Mansfield believed that he would be better off without someone at his side, the brass insisted the department work in pairs. Dave's previous associate had expired quickly, and although a significant amount of speculation around his death existed, the medical examiner's office ruled it a homicide. No one appeared interested in pursuing the death any further.

After starting his career with the MPD as a patrolman, Lance Sharpe rose to become a narcotics agent and then an execution inspector in 1997. At that point, he met Dave Mansfield, and things took a turn. Sharpe was clueless regarding what his future held.

According to the tale, in March 1999, the two detectives were investigating a shooting in the Tanglewood Place neighborhood, notorious for its high violent crime rate. Dave testified that a suspicious figure diverted his coworker from the determined direction of the search. When he heard gunshots, Dave went to find his companion and discovered Sharpe with a bullet in his skull. Mansfield sent a radio call for assistance, but his fellow worker passed at Jackson Memorial Hospital the next day.

Landers recalled the gossip about how the man died. Some supported manslaughter, while others accepted the suicide theory. The absence of evidence and witnesses made the case difficult for anybody to conclude. The assassination of Sharpe, only hours before he was due to testify in the South Miami Police Department Gang of Six court case, sparked many discussions.

The task force investigating this Gang of Six case was notorious for its corruption. After investigation, the authorities suspected them of colluding to conceal evidence, trafficking drugs, and intimidating citizens who refused to comply. Sharpe, suspected of participating, received a subpoena to testify, notwithstanding his denials of the accusations. The alleged murder and suicide rumors sprang from discussions surrounding this subpoena. Mike did not want to be the next dead colleague.

Paired with Mansfield for the past five years, Landers realized he misread the circumstances of Dave's previous associate. Mansfield was 14 years older than Landers, but he understood how to make the station's computers and operating systems sing and dance as the younger team member. He could romance Google with the best of them. Not only did Landers organize the investigative reports, but he also prepared most of the victimology material. Dave admired his ability to conduct in-depth analyses of complex topics for years.

Considering Mansfield's ongoing eating concerns, Landers began to discuss the case. "So, this morning, the father came up in our conversation. What can be learned from his publicized concert itinerary is that he spends a considerable amount of time away from home. On top of that, there's a studio apartment beyond the Angel Bluff property where he likely practices the piano. The one at Angel Bluff looked like it was never touched."

"That's one place we need to look into for sure," Mansfield noted. "Anyone contacted him yet?"

"Word is his manager called the precinct and asked for the person in charge of the case, and the operator sent him to Rita Slater. I guess she gave the notification. He is now on his way to the States, and patrol is scheduled to meet him when he arrives." Mansfield nodded his head. One less nasty job they needed to do, but he would have liked to gauge the man's reaction.

Landers resumed, "The mom worked as a real estate broker. When I say she worked, I mean she owned an agency and employed realtors. However, with an active license and a successful business, she must have also spent a good deal of time away from home. We should run by and take in what the rumor mill at the agency is saying." Mansfield shook his head in agreement.

"Seems as though the kids all but raised themselves. Have you learned anything useful about either of them?" Mansfield asked as he wiped his hands and mouth on a napkin and pushed his plate toward the center of the table.

"The boy was a shining star in the 6th grade and displayed exceptional academic and athletic capabilities. The school said he had a sharp mind and a thirst for knowledge, consistently surpassed academic expectations, and eagerly engaged in classroom discussions. Not only did he excel in academics, but he also demonstrated his athletic ability on the playing field, competing with passion and determination. He played on the school's soccer squad."

"However, the girl, Victoria, seemed to be an altogether different matter. Until this year, she was an enthusiastic learner who posted high grades. As a junior, she earned detention and spent time skipping school regularly," Landers answered.

"We did find that picture of what looked to be a boyfriend in her bedroom—kind of goth-like. I wonder if he was what was going on. It sounds like we need to make a trip to the school."

"I located the name of the last person she was texting with from her phone—22-year-old Luca Medina. The picture on the nightstand matched his driver's license, suggesting he was the boyfriend. We can follow up and figure out if he knows anything."

"Though tedious at times, going over the interview transcripts proved worthwhile. I found two things of note—the first morsel ties into what you are saying. The neighbor at 1618 Angel Bluff mentioned the family must have been having trouble with the daughter because she always sneaked in and out of her bedroom window."

"Another neighbor, the one across the street, said she noticed a suspicious car parked between the Moody's and the house on the other side for about 30 minutes before police arrived. Although the car was undoubtedly stolen, she described it as a newer version of a Nissan Maxima. She felt the car was dark but couldn't tell because of the heavy rain," Mansfield continued.

After lunch, the detectives returned to the station. Landers searched the stolen vehicle database to scan for any Nissan Maximas from recent years that disappeared within the last two weeks. A few unresolved Maximas popped up, but none were dark-colored within the surrounding metro area. This was information to be used later.

Mansfield went to Rita to ask about news on the arrival of Mark Moody. The time difference between Salzburg and Miami was approximately six hours, so he would lose six hours on his return flights. According to Slater, he would arrive at the airport at 7:00 pm. They planned for her to bring him to the bureau at 8:00 am the following morning.

Chapter 8

She struggled to catch her breath as she climbed out of the second-story window of her bedroom. Not from the cold or fatigue and certainly not from physical inability. From fear. Genuine fear. Victoria stood at the end of the driveway in the cool night air, knowing that her mother would kill her if she found out what she was doing.

Here she was, a 16-year-old girl sneaking out to meet a 22-year-old man she met on the Internet. Had she lost her mind? He needed to park his car at the end of the street, and she wondered if he could see her. The absence of proper street lighting made it unlikely.

Luca Medina met Victoria Moody online shortly after her 16th birthday. His most recent romance had been with a receptionist named Krystal, who was 17 years his senior. They broke up because Krystal feared Luca and his beliefs. During her conversations with Luca, Victoria learned that he had grown up in a rough area. At age two, his mother abandoned him, and all knew Dad as a drunkard. Victoria would have recognized this as an age-old tale if she had lived long enough.

Luca's pictures showed a handsome man of medium height with black hair and piercing green eyes. Victoria found herself in love, assuming internet pictures imitated real life. After a lifetime of keyboarding each other, they made plans to meet.

Victoria took a couple of steps toward the designated meeting place, and the wind gently stroked her hair and grazed her face comfortingly. This boosted her confidence and inspired her to keep going; she wanted excitement, risk, and danger in her otherwise dull existence. Despite her trembling legs, she continued to walk, taking ragged breaths as she drew closer to the crossroad.

"Hello, Vicki," a baritone voice said. Vicki believed he must have seen the astonishment register on her face before she was able to suppress it since she spotted a faint smile split his lips. The amazement wasn't in what he said. His words were like vanilla ice cream, sweet and ordinary, but the richness of his tones—sumptuous and warm, smooth chocolate all the way. A larger man's voice, but somehow fit him perfectly.

"Hey, Luca," Vicki answered as she reached the car's driver's side. A god-like Luca stepped out of the vehicle, and Vicki questioned why she had landed there that night. Things became apparent as soon as he opened the passenger door for her. Destiny and fate controlled chance, allowing her to leap toward a life she had always anticipated.

Luca put the car in gear and asked, "What time do you need to return?" He glanced over at Vicki with a reassuring grin.

"No one knows I'm gone. My mom and brother are sleeping, and my dad is out of town. I'm golden unless one of them wakes up. I shouldn't be gone too long," Vicki responded, keeping her voice as strong as possible, even though her legs continued to wobble a bit.

"Very well, I know a little cafe right up the street. We can go for a piece of pie and coffee. How's that?"

"Perfect." She became aware of the music playing on the car stereo while driving. Vicki listened closely as the melancholy sounds were bleak with solid undertones of sorrow. From what she could decipher, the vocalist sang about a vampire who decided not to consume blood but sought ultimate death instead. A little odd but captivating.

"What is this music? Are they talking about vampires?" Vicki blurted out.

"Dark Wave. I'd tell you about the genre, but you'd think I was a crow. Some call it Gothic Rock, but when you can take the time to listen, there is something quite distinct from Gothic Rock. I can put something else on?"

"Oh no. It's chill."

Upon arrival, Vicki noted that the few guests at Paul's Front Porch Cafe were dressed in punk rock styles, and Luca fit right in when he stepped out of the vehicle. She, unfortunately, was sure she appeared square as hell with her materialism and aloofness, like every other kid from Angel Bluff—a total outsider in this neighborhood.

Her eyes flashed with all the excitement of a pig sneaking into a fat farm. Her hands twisted tightly, and her teeth bit down on her lower lip. Thankfully, this panic only lasted until Luca grabbed her hand, told her she was bangin', and walked with her into the coffee shop.

Vicki spent the rest of the summer immersed in Luca and his world. His subculture had a rigid code of ethics and several regulations, which she found easy and logical. Luca made his living as a DJ for parties and nightclubs, which is the reason he had so much knowledge of music and the industry. The people she met were content with their lives, status, and friends. Conversations covered many topics and seldom focused on money, as they always did at Angel Bluff, and Vicki found this to be a welcome change.

She discovered many visitors seemed dissatisfied as she submerged further into the community. She concluded that feeling restless, unsatisfied, and envious of others was a regular aspect of being human. Yet, these unhappy people found themselves terrified of change. She saw this every day at the Moody residence. It didn't take long before Vicki dressed like the others and became a part of the community. She related to their values.

One week before her junior year of high school began, Vicki experienced her 'first encounter'. She was shopping with Luca at the Twisted Shadow, where the owner knew Luca well, and, as Vicki's introduction finished, a middle-aged woman with two teenage boys walked through the door. The woman approached the three and threw a false smile. Vicki immediately detected the incongruity. *It is in the eyes*, she thought to herself. *They are just a bit too shiny, or is it the smile itself, a touch too bright, too wide? Something's off.*

Vicki glanced at Luca to catch his reaction. None. Her senses told her this person's smile did not fit, and it made her extremely anxious. *Is she smiling at something of which I am not aware? Something is going on.* She glanced at Luca and again at the woman. There was more pleasure or wit than the situation called for—and it was not necessarily good. *The woman relished something, but what?*

"Hello, all. I guess that time of year has arrived again." She opened her lips covered in a matte dark red lipstick and revealed teeth that had all been filed to a point, like an animal's teeth. After the teeth, Vicki took in the details of the vintage long-waisted deep red vest with the cavernous V neckline. The tight-fitting embossed leather had a subtle rose design and steel boning to help maintain its shape. Had she worn a full A-line black tulle skirt with layers of mesh overlay, Vicki would have thought she was dressing for a party and going as a goth queen.

Nevertheless, she wore the tightest-fitting black leather skinny pants with black heels, making her appear to be a size four with two children. Her abundant raven black hair was partially pulled into a messy bun, and she carried a headband with maleficent horns and gothic black roses. She added two twigs of black leaves, which she gathered around the back of the roses. Vicki almost blundered into fitful laughter.

"Yes, it is," replied Luca in a friendly but formal manner, almost bowing from the waist. "Well, Vicki, let's be about our business." Vicki smiled at the group as she and Luca walked off, leaving the woman and her kids to speak with the store manager.

"Little girl, you really should let your nails grow out, or at least invest in some fakes, because your striking personality isn't the first thing people see," the woman said to Vicki as they walked off. Vicki started to turn around and engage the woman, but Luca had a death grip on her elbow and kept her walking in a direction away from them.

Vicki turned to Luca, "What does she mean by that? What does she mean by 'that time of year again'?"

"She is talking about shopping for school clothes. It's no big deal for you because you wear a uniform. I'm sure your mom shops for Cooper's school clothes. She also keeps your uniform up-to-date and size-appropriate."

"Oh, right! School. Hey, I recognized those kids. What's wrong with their mom's grill, and why is she dressed like that?"

Luca slowed his gait and looked over compassionately at Vicki. He looked into her eyes and whispered, "Now, watch your reaction." He paused to make sure he had her attention. "They are vampires."

Chapter 9

"Hello, Ms. Parsons," Landers began after standing back to read the receptionist's nameplate. "I realize it's been a difficult day, but we're with Miami PD and would like to speak with someone in management concerning Ms. Moody's death."

She glanced at Landers, wondering if he was speaking in an alien language from *Star Wars*, and she prepared to take her time answering. Her glossed-over, moist eyes cleared slightly when she looked at Mansfield. The millennial's look offered flattering praise but didn't last long.

"I have worked at Trendsetter for almost two years and loved every minute. Ya, get me?" She started whimpering, staring down at the daily Miami Herald in front of her. "These days, Ms. Moody would participate only in the big deals. She came and went as she wanted. Evie became my all-time favorite boss within a week. Well, she was the only boss I've experienced. Do I still have a job?"

"Carol and Kisha are the top sellers and the only ones who care about the place. You should talk to them." She looked at Mansfield and blinked her eyes pathetically. Landers shook his head, and Mansfield reminded him that slapping her was just not worth jail time.

The top agents each received their own office. Many similar cubicles, with only half walls arranged in a horizontal and vertical pattern in the center of the room, left a geometric impression—a minimalist look like Ms. Moody's personal domicile. Nothing personal could be seen. Carol and Kisha occupied offices along the inside wall of the primary bullpen.

Mansfield stopped to speak to Carol, who occupied the closest office to the receptionist. After introducing himself and allowing Carol to gather herself, Carol gave the detective a history of her work at the agency. She became Evie's first hired agent, and they learned how the business worked.

"We worked our butts off trying to meet people, make connections, and fit into the community. Evie became a natural, and because of her skills, the business took off, and we were making good money. Then she married Mark and decided to have children. That's when Kisha started. The company grew, and as a team, we were making more money than we ever dreamed," Carol beamed.

"Can you think of anyone who would want to hurt Ms. Moody? Is it possible a bargain went south, or someone felt duped?" Mansfield asked, confident this woman had a hidden agenda.

"I can't say I do," Carol answered, folding her hands and putting them in her lap. Mansfield sat there momentarily and let the silence gnaw at her insides. He was aware of the stillness that engulfed the office like a gaping void, needing to be filled with sounds, words, anything. It was poisonous in its nothingness, cruelly underscoring how pointless their conversation had been thus far.

For some reason, Mansfield couldn't help but marvel at how this woman could be a top salesperson in Miami's most exclusive neighborhoods. She showed little personality; her clothing made her look like she belonged on the television show *Little House on the Prairie*, and to put it in the words of his youth, she was a butterface. When Carol spoke, her voice trailed, making it sound like her words were unwilling to make the journey.

"Well, Evie's stellar reputation preceded her. She was crafty and, when called for, ruthless. As her kids got older and demanded less of her, she returned to full-time work although she avoided selling activities. She mainly concentrated on the bureaucratic and community relations facets of the job."

"She and Mark grew further apart as his career took off, and she had a couple of affairs. She hired a lawyer and was preparing to file for divorce." Carol finally finished, looking mournful but secretly satisfied with herself.

"I'm sorry she was so troubled. Do you recall whom she saw this last time?"

"No. She would leave in the afternoons to meet him."

"Carol, are you aware if she discussed divorce with her husband or served him papers before he left on this last trip?" Mansfield continued to push for answers.

"No. She'd been so indifferent recently. One time, I spotted a file on her desk, which indicated the documents were completed. Mark would make his way back to the house occasionally, but she may not have addressed it yet." Carol shook her head and looked down at her folded hands. "My guess is Evie had enough of this lifestyle and was preparing to leave the country."

"Why would she do that?" Mansfield worked to control his tone; this was one of the things about his job he hated, even though it always paid off. He could only take so much of the phony sorrow and distress people like Carol thought they needed to display when they only wanted to share the victim's dirty secrets. They reminded him of foul weeds in an otherwise well-kept garden.

"She didn't get along with her daughter for many reasons, and she often said Mark needed to take responsibility for Cooper. I think she wanted to shed the baggage and go somewhere to start all over, where nobody knew her."

Meanwhile, Landers interviewed Kisha in an office further down the hall, who better understood the day's events than the receptionist. Kisha earned the title of top seller although she joined the team well after it was established.

"Listen, Evie was a rainmaker. She was charismatic, socially adept, and a networker with a large circle of connections and a big ego, which she parlayed into an excellent reputation," Kisha summarized. "She had no qualms about putting in the work necessary to achieve her goals."

"What do you mean by that?" Landers asked.

"I mean, she could make the hard choices. She was a negotiator and understood the art of the deal. She put a value on everything, so when things needed to be handled outside of the law or inside of the bedroom, she considered it all part of the equation." Landers thought Kisha might have been describing herself instead of Evie.

Shaking his head to communicate understanding, Landers pushed forward, "Are you aware of anyone who would want to hurt Ms. Moody? It might be a bad deal or someone who thought the math did not work out." He was pretty impressed with Kisha's forthrightness.

"The first person that comes to mind would be her husband. She was filing for divorce, which would severely diminish his net worth. But more than that, if she died, he would assume ownership of Trendsetter, the whole exquisite enterprise," Kisha offered as she leaned back in her chair and interlocked her fingers playfully.

"Do you have any idea why she wanted a divorce?"

"Why does any woman file? She had some action on the side; he was always gone; it's her money; I can continue if you like. She started showing interest in a same-sex relationship in the past year, though. Made her a bit more human."

"Is this a fact or a feeling? I mean, seeing someone of the same sex regularly?"

"I wouldn't say it is a fact, but I'm pretty sure. The person is related somehow to one of her kids. She was on the phone not long ago talking about meeting up after the game." Kisha shrugged to indicate whatever that meant.

The detectives surveyed Evie's office. Mansfield counted exactly five things on her desk: a computer, mouse, planner, pen, and reading glasses. Nothing of personal value adorned the walls or bookcases. Two file cabinets stood in the far corner, and two chairs sat in front of the desk. That was the sum of the office.

Mansfield raised one eyebrow and shook his head, "Again, we witness Ms. Moody's minimalist personality. It seems to show up in every aspect of her life."

"It sure does," Landers responded. "She probably had high traits of discipline. I bet she thrived on structure and planning. A very political animal." Landers walked around the desk, opening drawers while Mansfield opened the planner.

Landers found a file with correspondence of the divorce, and Mansfield found several brochures for European countries. The detectives took the file and the planner with them when they left.

Chapter 10

Freedom Pointe's 25-acre campus included assisted living facilities, a small commercial area, and an independent living complex. The grounds contained 20 freestanding cabins and high-rise apartments. To travel about the property, the residents relied on golf carts. Each cottage had a golf cart, creating one of the most exciting aspects of living at Freedom Pointe. When it came time to hang up their license, some seniors knew better than others, but never once did giving up the golf cart cross their minds!

After the interviews at Trendsetter, Mansfield popped a couple of pain pills to dull the throbbing of his tooth socket and jumped on West Flagler Street, then drove to his mother's place for dinner. Several factors made this visit so challenging, including the distance and traffic. She sometimes called, laid on much guilt, and set up a time for them to have an annoying and uncomfortable visit.

She always wanted him in politics and would not be happy until he gave up his blue-collar life and became a political figure. After a day like today, dining with her was the last thing he wanted to do, but he worried for his elderly mother. After his father passed years ago, she sold their home and furnishings in Washington D.C., took the equity—not as much as she hoped for—added it to her investments, and moved to sunny Miami.

Jackie Mansfield's go-to outfit included a pair of stilettos and a tailored pantsuit. Small steps were her trademark, and she adored the sound of her arrival being proclaimed by the click-click-click. Every snow-white hair on her 84-year-old head had been sprayed, rendering it immovable and immobile. Permanently tattooed on her face, her make-up remained flawless.

Besides her crimson rouge lips, she had arched brown eyebrows that leaped at the chance to communicate. She used a cosmetic blusher to accentuate her cheekbones and spent a substantial chunk of her monthly income on wrinkle treatments to appear younger. Yes, she was vain; most people could pick her out of a crowd.

Jackie dominated the conversation with her thoughts regarding the election results. All negative, of course. Listening to her denounce George W. Bush and his handling of the September 11 attacks in 2001 and the invasion of Afghanistan reminded Mansfield of the purgatory called his college years. It was all old information to him.

She argued that Bush's re-election was a political lightning rod and the worst thing that could have happened to America. She droned on, and Dave remembered why he did not care much about his parents' political stance on matters. The dinner parties with other politicians he attended when he was younger became increasingly unpalatable, and the more he learned, the less he cared for their friends. Dave viewed the people and parties as a coalition of social factions, each seeking government intervention and action.

It seemed to him that the government should decrease taxes, a capitalist economy should thrive, immigration limits should be put in place, and military expenditures should be considered normal. Then, as now, he burned inside with argument. However, he remained stoic and detached, careful not to show emotion.

He glanced around the dining hall as Jackie remained self-absorbed in her conversation. The residents of Freedom Pointe were more than capable of providing entertainment. However, grumpy Allen, who typically sat by the window and made such a big deal of eating his soup, was missing again tonight. Allen's wife died about two and a half years ago, and now he ate alone, mostly making a big mess.

"Hey, Mom, where is Allen tonight? The last few times I've been here, he has been nowhere to be seen," Dave interrupted her diatribe.

"Oh, he got so bad they transferred him to assisted living. He couldn't even hold the silverware anymore and always made too big of a mess. It became too disgusting having him in the dining hall," Jackie complained.

"Ray seems pretty calm. What's the matter with him?" Dave asked to keep his mom from returning to her political rhetoric. Ray was a gruff, foul-mouthed 90-something-year-old with a terrible temper who always bellyached over anything.

"Ray, oh son, this is juicy. Ray's latest girlfriend got sick and went to the hospital. Doctors diagnosed Chlamydia in her throat, so they say. Isn't that gross? Her daughter became so furious that she removed her mother right away from Freedom Pointe, and I think they plan to sue the place," Jackie beamed with the news.

"Did they test Ray also?"

"He refused to let them. No noticeable symptoms, and they can't force him to take the test. So he's been lying low, no one to show off for."

As Jackie finished, a well-dressed senior stopped by the table and smiled at the two. "Jackie, it is so nice to see you. This must be your son you've told me so much about." The man looked over to Dave and nodded his head. He then looked back at Jackie with bright eyes dancing with mischief. Jackie looked up at the man and blushed, much in a younger woman's manner. Dave soon recognized the intense eye contact and was astounded by the effect on his mother—a true master of charm.

"Caspar, you always surprise me," Jackie gathered herself. "Yes, this is my son, Dave. He is here checking up on me as all good children do." Jackie smiled at Dave and patted him on the hand.

Dave stood to shake Caspar's hand. "Please excuse me. I underwent dental surgery this morning and still feel the effects. It's a pleasure to meet you, Caspar. Would you like to join us?" Dave offered. His warm handshake made Dave want to wipe his hand over the front of his slacks.

"No, no, thank you. I just finished and am on my way out. I wanted to stop by and say hello to the beautiful Jackie Mansfield before I retire for the evening." Caspar bent at the waist a bit, nodded toward Jackie, and left. Dave sat down speechless.

After observing his mother, he discovered she was content there. When first arriving at Freedom Pointe, she struggled to find activities that she felt comfortable participating in. It was easier for her to play Canasta because she only needed to navigate her way with three inmates at a time. She found other ladies who became her close friends, and soon Jackie, Maggie, Bee, and Donna were inseparable. However, watching her with Caspar, Dave could see her self-confidence and that she could make her own decisions. She remained an independent individual who was not easily influenced by the opinions of others—a true reflection of her self-identity.

"So how is the Canasta crowd doing?" Dave probed, not wanting to linger about Caspar. "Are you and Bee still beating up on everyone?"

Over the years, Bee became Jackie's best friend and her regular Canasta partner. Mansfield checked in regularly on his mother's relationship with Bee because of a dangerous situation the two of them found themselves in years ago due to Bee's son, Thomas Blair. Although the world's events have rumbled forward since then, the cartels still circled like vultures above a tottering camel.

"Everyone is doing great," Jackie replied. "Donna is having health issues and missing many games because of chemotherapy. But we picked up another player, Flora, who plays with us when Donna doesn't feel like it."

"I'm sorry to learn Donna hasn't been doing well. Is Thomas in touch with Bee very much?" Dave inquired casually.

"He calls sometimes. He made a few visits to her cabin and removed some stuff he had stored there. It looks much better without all those antiques sitting around everywhere. I can't wait for him to get all of them out. I want her to be safer."

"Does he come and get them or bring other people?" Dave was interested because he didn't want anyone to know Bee had valuables in her cabin.

"Bee said he generally drops by at night by himself. However, a few times, she's seen a car parked across the street with people in it. Just parked, doing nothing. She thinks they are the same type of thugs she saw in the back of the shop with the bags of cash, and it makes her a little nervous. They aren't always parked, just occasionally."

"Did she report this to Peter Ekker at the DEA office? Is she making a list of when she sees the car and for how long it stays?" Dave asked, concerned that she might be compromised.

"I don't know," Jackie fretted.

"Mom, you need to talk with Bee and find out. If she hasn't contacted Peter yet, she must do this immediately. If she hasn't started keeping a log, she must also start doing this promptly," Dave reached over and patted his mother's hand. "Do you understand me, Mom? This is important. If she does not want to do this, call me so that I can track Peter down."

Chapter 11

By 1969, the communist regime erected dozens of children's houses and embarked on a campaign to present them as a viable alternative to the traditional family. The message to parents remained simple: the state can care for your child better than you can. By this time, state orphanages housed thousands of children who had been given over to the state or seized from their parents.

Yetta's baby boy was first sent to the children's house in Bucharest. The nurses immediately disliked him because of his darkness. When the child opened his eyes, they all scattered, stating he had demons. To keep him from glaring at them as they performed the required activities of feeding and changing, they would frequently apply bandages to his eyes.

He soon became known as the Suflet Intunecat, the Romanian term for Dark Soul. For the first year, Suflet Intunecat fed in the dresser drawer that acted as his crib, and he received a generous diaper change once a day. He remained separated from the other infants and was taken to a facility in Brasov for the handicapped. With his deformed development pattern and heightened sensitivity to light, Suflet Intunecat proved extremely fortunate to have survived the Bucharest hellhole.

Found off the beaten path, only some knew the institution in Brasov existed. Outer barriers obscured a multi-story building where youngsters moved from floor to floor as they matured. Children experienced no outside activities, no gymnasium, no pool, and few windows. To look at the complex was to see old Romanian walls with remnants of former greatness.

There was no indication that hundreds of children deemed unsalvageable lived in an unmarked structure behind the walls. The castle-like look of the facility and the stench of standing water had become the property's most striking features.

Once inside, the stone enclosure was filled with the sickening stench of sulfur and the chilly breezes that moved through it like the long-reaching fingers of aged ghosts. Additionally, the fragrance of boiled cabbage cooked too long permeated the halls; its odor multiplied until it burned the noses of individuals unaccustomed.

Those with keener olfactory receptors would detect a more complex perfume of decay and decomposition. The entire impression left a bitter taste in the back of one's mouth. However, the goal was not to make good impressions but to thin out these marked souls as swiftly as possible. As a result, sexual abuse and beatings occurred daily.

Over the years, nurses and staff chiefly ignored Suflet Intunecat because they feared him. It took him a long time to become self-sufficient, considering how many starving and neglected children crowded every usable space. He was better off than those tethered to rusting metal cots or confined in cages.

The boy was not as developmentally delayed as most thought, and he never spoke when staff members could overhear. He mainly survived on meals of boiled cabbage and meager portions of bread and cheese.

He spent many hours rocking back and forth, clutching himself, and looking out the tallest window he could reach. He grew fond of the scents of trees picked up by the wind. On rare occasions, he caught whiffs from nearby places like wood smoke or stagnant pools of water.

In the distance, he could see a castle atop a low mountain. The castle belonged to the district of Transylvania, with the town of Bran at the foot, but Suflet Intunecat did not understand geography. What he did know about this castle built on the side of the mountain was that the staff said extreme horrors took place there. Horror that made what happened in this house seem inconsequential. Staff members talked about how Vlad the Impaler lived in that castle. It took time for him to appreciate what they were talking about, but he didn't want anything to do with it once he got it.

Also, within his purview was a cabin on the side of a hill much closer to the orphanage. A man, a woman, and five children lived in this house, which was close enough to touch. The man left early every day and returned just before dark. For years, Suflet Intunecat considered what the children did outside with each other and why their mother brought food outside.

The family became very predictable, and Suflet Intunecat grew to hate them, even though he wanted to be part of them. As time passed, he became passionate about leaving the only home he knew and going out into the world to be with his new family.

Suflet Intunecat turned 13 and began to prepare for his escape. The complex was a prison despite the absence of bars on the windows and dozens of guards patrolling the periphery. The time eventually came, and when everyone was eating their final meal for the day, Suflet Intunecat picked a pair of shoes out of a communal trunk, put on a coat, and scooped up his sleeping rags.

He went on his way. No one stayed at the gate this late, and he had no trouble opening and shutting it after he left. Making the distance to the wooded area was what mattered now. The sun began to dip below the horizon, casting a golden glow over the castle's walls, and this adventurous soul swiftly navigated through the rugged terrain, dodging gnarled roots and leaping over misplaced stones, his destination hidden amidst the embrace of the darkening woods.

The sky rapidly plunged into threatening darkness, waking predatory creatures into the night. Suflet Intunecat jumped as a distant bloodcurdling howl made his arms and legs tingle and his palms instantly sweated. He hunched down as he witnessed the woods transform into a deadly playground for animals he never imagined existed.

Tree branches stretched before him to reach out and grab his flesh. It was time to move, to run fast and far. The tree branches were getting longer by the minute and gained on him. It wasn't long before an awful pain spread throughout his chest like a deadly infection, and his lungs demanded he could go no further.

After running for so long, his knees turned to rubber, and now he gulped selfish breaths of air. Earthy and beastly aromas enveloped him. Helpless to do anything else, he walked on, his feet shuffling noisily through the twigs and fallen leaves beneath him, each step rustling the animals rooting in the underbrush and triggering a rush of pain in his chest.

Despite his weak condition, Suflet Intunecat curled his lips into a smile as the realization that he had finally escaped struck him. Finally, free of the grasp of the oppressive government, he bathed in his victory.

He thought about the place he saw when he peered back over his shoulder once he got to the tree line. The place looked nothing like he thought. It resembled a castle like the one on the hill. The castle walls rose out of the darkness, out of the silent charcoal curtain called dusk. The wall was pitted and desolate, never to be the bastion of protection and glory castles were meant to be.

By now, his body heat did not so much as drain away or leach out slowly; it abandoned him with callous speed to leave him helpless and shivering too violently to continue fleeing. He had an overwhelming temptation to hide right where he stood. How quickly the dream of the runaway had become a nightmare. However, he was free.

Chapter 12

At the time, he was just 15 years old with black wavy hair and a light complexion; he stood tall and lean. Despite the filth, sadness, and drought, Mark went to school as an ordinary student, yet he became the state's top performer on the standardized state test for tenth graders. Mark Moody also played a raging piano and stunned audiences with his skills. Even at this early age, he deeply loved the piano and often lost himself in music. Comfortable with his abilities, it wasn't uncommon for him to volunteer to play piano with any band that came to town to perform at the Fortress Theater. Mark envisioned himself leveraging his abilities as a pianist to one day escape the dust and gravel roads of South Dakota.

Mark's father coached football at the high school. As a part of the school community, he sincerely cared about his players' well-being. He could successfully convey football concepts to his players because of his extensive coaching experience. He was a well-organized coach who followed through on his practice plans regularly. It's no surprise, therefore, that the high school football team had consistent success throughout the years.

Mark, unfortunately, fell short of every hope his father had for him. His father preferred youngsters with power, speed, athletic talent, and the ability to learn the game fast, according to his system. Mark's attributes focused on creativity, tenacity, patience, and sensitivity. From the moment Mark took a breath, the two were at odds.

The death of Mark's mother had a profound effect on his life. Once she entered labor, his father ordered him to find a midwife. No doctors or hospitals for the coach's household; everything happened in the old ways. Mark did not return in time, and the mother and the baby perished. His father blamed him for their deaths and, in his rage, took a kitchen knife to Mark.

To this day, the piano player sports a scar on the right middle finger that he received from the incident. Mark's father abandoned him after the conflict.

The man mourned, and as a result, he became detached and self-absorbed, unwilling to give importance to Mark and his emotional agony. His father sent him to the midwife too late, and Mark became angrier as he thought about it. Mark hopped a freight train to escape the anguish and sorrow over his father's recklessness, never to return.

An older Mark Moody walked into the police station promptly, escorted by Officer Rita Slater at 8:00 am. His wavy black hair was now flecked with gray around the temples. The whiskers that graced his square jaw were a stubby ashen color with an unkempt cultivated quality. The entire package had a distinct and seductive vibe about it. He could see it all over Rita's subtle actions. Mansfield thought it might be because he was comfortable and confident in his skin.

"Hello, Mr. Moody. I'm Detective Mansfield. I want to offer my condolences on your loss and thank you for coming in to speak with me," Mansfield began, offering Mark a seat at the interview table. "I understand you flew in from Austria last night. I'm sorry you could not go home, but the house is still a crime scene. I assume your accommodation was acceptable."

"Fine, as expected," Mark said as he sat opposite Mansfield. He rubbed one hand against the scarred wood table, his fingertips stumbling across the mutilation that spoiled the illusion of normalcy. Nothing made sense anymore; the table, chair, and dingy walls were without direction and meaning.

Mark stared at the detective who stood there and considered him. His children and wife would be gone if the detective was correct. What happened that the rest of the world was still here? He wished the world would dissolve around him, but when he glanced down, he still noticed the scarred wood and the coolness of the air that refused to allow the screaming anguish that tore through his body to release itself. His insides became emotionless without warning, and he looked up at Detective Mansfield.

"When can I visit my family?" Mark asked with an unwavering tone while looking directly into the detective's eyes. He flattened his downward palms, fingers straightened, and stretched back in his chair. Mansfield recognized intelligence under the mask of confidence, but something in his eyes told a different tale.

"After our quick interview, we can escort you to the morgue, so you can formally identify the bodies," Mansfield answered. Landers and Officer Slater stood in the observation room watching the interview. In a gesture of nonverbal communication, Mansfield placed both hands in sight by laying them in front of him, palms up. He hoped this would help ease the man's stiffness, which had just emerged.

"Mr. Moody, are you away from home on tours frequently?" Mansfield asked casually.

"Well, that's not an easy question to answer. It depends on how many concerts my agent books for the year. More performances mean more rehearsals and time to learn the deficiencies and challenges of the crap pianos with which I am expected to make magic." Mansfield gave Mark a perplexed look.

"Oh man, come on. Think about it. I don't transport my piano to every concert, as other musicians do with smaller instruments. I expect a certain degree of excellence with the piano provided, but no piano is flawless, and each has an individual personality, much like a woman." Mark roughly tapped the last three fingers of his right hand on the tabletop as he educated the detective on the obvious points of being a world-renowned pianist.

"However, I do book downtime. I need time to work on scales, practice new pieces, write music, and unwind. During those times, I am in town." Mark's tone shifted as he choked back his anger.

"Yes, the piano in your house is fantastic. You must have practiced when the children went to school, and the wife was at the agency." Mansfield waited for Moody to reveal the flat.

"Oh no. I would never attempt to compose in that dreadfully unpleasant house. Who could ever create genius from such insanity? I have a studio apartment where I can be spontaneous, laugh, keep my soul light, and my mind can function as our creator intended. Through my creative endeavors in music, I keep my mind open, and it is exhausting!"

"Then sleep comes like the falling of an ax. I know it must come, but I fight it with everything I have. In those defenseless hours, oblivious to everything around me, my entire body lights up with fiery sparks. Then I crash."

"Sleep is as instantaneous as it is unwelcome. There is no time to drive home. I barely make it to the bed, just in the next room. It takes a while before I feel I can rejoin the world again," Mark responded.

"That's great you have a place to work where you are comfortable. Can I have that address?" Moody had no difficulty sharing this information and wrote the address on a paper pad for the detective. Mansfield knew the address, but he wanted Mark to give it to him.

Mansfield reflected while Moody wrote, "Did either of the kids play the piano at the house? Did either of them want to follow you?"

"Absolutely not. Cooper is all about sports. He has his grandfather's genetics. Those genes skipped over me. My son thinks I'm worthless because I won't play catch or kick around a ball with him. I tell him that is what friends and coaches are for."

"And Victoria has no hobbies or interests. She used to be into academics and school, but she opted out this year. She started hanging around a less desirable crowd; as I understand it, she is hardly ever home. I think her mother likes it that way, as long as she gets Cooper where he needs to be when he needs to be there." Moody was detached in his speech, as though he was talking about someone else's family.

Mansfield noted that Moody spoke of the family in the present tense. He did not appear nervous or scared, but he did seem a bit bipolar. Moody had offered much of the information he knew about the children and their circumstances. The only thing left to discuss was his marriage, which could be sensitive.

"So, Mark, may I call you Mark?" Moody shook his head in agreement. "After 17 years of marriage, how was your relationship with your wife? Did your absence impact your marriage?" This was a key driver behind Mansfield's hunt for a rationale to guide the investigation in a specific direction. Mark Moody's answer was all he needed now. Would it be the angry Moody or the confident Moody?

Landers and Slater inhaled deeply as Mansfield laid out the question. Both remained glued to the one-sided glass window, eagerly awaiting Moody's response. Time froze while they waited. Moody's face twitched as his chest rose and fell irregularly while they observed him.

Moody's anxiety erupted as he began tapping the last three fingers on the tabletop as he had done before. Mansfield looked over at the tapping fingers and silently waited. The morning promised to stretch before them like a long winding road. Mansfield took stock of this man. His eyes resembled those of a disturbing statue.

"Meaningful connections are built over time; it's no wonder so many of us have so few of them. Matrimony never provides everything; it only provides some things. As a man, you pick the things you want from a marriage—say, sexual chemistry, enjoyable conversation, or loyalty, and the rest of your needs must be handled elsewhere. Isn't it clear that this is a trap?" Moody pleaded.

"Trying to find everything in a marriage would be useless." Moody articulated the punch line with a solemn expression. Again, he had lashed out with hazy words—this time in earnest.

Mansfield gave the predetermined signal, resulting in a knock on the door. A young officer in uniform cracked the door slightly and asked for the detective. Mansfield walked to the door, and the officer whispered into his ear while sneaking glances in Mark's direction, as instructed.

Mansfield also looked over to Mark and whispered loudly, "I gotcha." Then both the officer and the detective exited the interview room, leaving Mr. Moody to his curiosity.

Chapter 13

Bobby pondered calling the cops and telling them what he knew, but he didn't know what to say. If the cops asked him to describe the assailant, his only comment would be that the killer resembled everyone and no one. Bobby only presumed the killer was a man with what looked like black hair because he only saw him from the back, and the hair blended in with the dark clothes. The killer had been neither tall nor short enough to think about height; he had not been fat or thin enough to note weight or build. The more Bobby deliberated, even the person's race—whether White, Black, or Hispanic—was a mystery to him. Yes, with a story like this, he was suspect number one.

This Thursday morning, Archer was to be released from the hospital. Bobby spent most of yesterday planning the various situations in which he would get arrested when he left his residence and arrived at the hospital. Most of them centered around the description of his car.

These anxious thoughts were like going around the block repeatedly, accelerating progressively with each lap. It served no useful purpose. Bobby threw himself on the sofa and covered his head with a pillow. *If you act like a damn car, then let your thoughts be a car on a good road, taking the hills and valleys just the same. You owe it to yourself to take control of the wheel.* He mentally chastised himself. Then he rose to his feet carefully. He had the answer.

After getting dressed, Bobby exited his home to head to Archer's house, a few blocks away. He could have easily walked but wasn't experiencing his usual enthusiasm this morning. Instead, he made his way to a bus stop other than the one in front of his house by walking through the back alley.

It wasn't quite your picturesque alley, more of a pragmatic shortcut frequented by dogs, cats, people without housing, and anyone aiming to reach the back of the strip mall on the main road. Bobby deliberately tried to evade prying eyes as he maneuvered through numerous potholes, each harboring an unpleasant surprise. Unfortunately, he found himself gracefully gliding into one of those delightful abysses.

The air was heavy with the scent of decomposing fast-food wrappers and the remnants of a diaper, a tragic casualty of some untamed creature's mischief. As he pressed forward, an unwelcome bouquet of feline urine invaded his senses, accompanied by the sight of a formidable vomit pile. His upper lip curled, and he instinctively covered his nose and mouth, his breath slowing in response. Casting another wary glance around, Bobby found himself enveloped in an eerie stillness. A wave of claustrophobia washed over him, an unfamiliar sensation. In sheer determination, he embraced his inner Olympic sprinter and dashed his way to the open expanse beyond.

Assured no one cared about him, he boarded the bus that would take him around the block and down the street to Archer's residence. He overheard two men discussing the Angel Bluff killings on the bus. They said the father arrived home, and the police had him at the station for an interview. They felt for the man, coming home and having his entire family annihilated.

During their three minutes on the bus, Bobby kept his ears peeled for new information. Both men exited the bus at the next stop, and Bobby sat back in his seat and took a deep breath. Given his day, he was thirsty and ready to stop for a drink. *Concentrate*, he kept telling himself. *Concentrate on what you're doing.* At Archer's place, Bobby found the keys to Archer's unassuming Ford truck, which, unlike his car, was older, and even more unimpressive, and no one was looking for it.

Inside the hospital, Bobby went directly to Archer's room and arrived to overhear the discharge instructions. The hospital room reminded Bobby of a concrete box with a window the size of a biscuit tin lid and an unpleasant stink, as though it had been cleaned with plain water rather than antiseptic.

The bed sat low to the ground, the frame displaying recent signs of corrosion, and the mattress dangerously thin. Bobby bit his lip. It was unthinkable to leave, and staying was sure to be a nightmare in its infancy. Before he even entered the room, a song began playing softly in his head, … *Welcome to the Hotel California…*

According to the nurse, "You should not be by yourself. You need a friend to stay with you until you return to normal. Do not drink alcoholic beverages and avoid strenuous activities. Do not drive or operate heavy machinery until the doctor clears you. Initially, you may experience mild headaches, depression, difficulty concentrating, or dizziness. These symptoms can last days to weeks."

As the nurse continued to talk, Bobby absorbed the room. It lacked attractiveness, and its walls were just cream, not peeling or unclean, but cream. Separated from the other three beds in the space, Archer's bed was next to insipid curtains that, at one time, may have been the type of green that evoked thoughts of spring and hope but had now faded to where the color was uninspiring.

There were no flowers, cards, or food sent in from home for the infirmed, and to fill the time, they either napped or stared into space. Bobby counted the stands for intravenous drips and monitors. Yep, one for each bed. Outside the door were dispensers for rubber gloves, hand sanitizer, and soap. He wondered if anyone used them.

At this point, the nurse spotted Bobby and responded, "Archer, you told me you didn't have any friends. And here, someone has come to drive you home. You are such a tease."

She then continued, this time with Bobby in mind, "Contact us if he has persistent nausea or vomiting, increased confusion, dizziness, trouble walking or staggering, convulsions, worsening headache, blood drainage from his ears or nose, or double vision." She finished with a polite smile.

Able to talk to Archer for the first time once they climbed into the truck, Bobby said, "So how are you doing, man? You look much better. Are you ready to escape and go home?"

"I had to be cautious. You only know half of it. I am glad you came. Who sent you? I kept quiet and did not say much of anything since I woke up. They never stopped probing me about where I was, what I was doing, who else was there when I fell, whatever. But I did not answer even one of their questions."

Bobby listened attentively, trying to understand what Archer meant to say. "Are you talking about the police? Did detectives come by and try to talk to you?"

"They disguised themselves in many ways. Did I tell you about the ones who steal? They come in at night and take my saliva. Sometimes they steal hair from my head or clip at my nails. It is the DNA they want to take—to make the clones. That is what happened to my family. Those people on the other beds you thought were my family are not my family; they are clones," Archer whispered loudly.

"Archer, I did not see your family. Your family died years ago. Do you want to go to the cemetery to see their graves?"

"Who are you, man? They lay right there in the room, in beds 2, 3, and 4. Mom, Dad, and my sister, Jennifer," Archer answered as he turned to give Bobby a quizzical look. Bobby continued to drive slowly and bit the thumbnail on his left hand. Turning around and taking Archer back would not do any good. Bobby was sure if he stood close enough to Archer, the ocean's roar would be audible.

Bobby had known Archer for going on 10 years. He was the old hermit who lived down the street. Bobby would take short walks, and it became clear that Archer only ventured out of his trailer occasionally, most of the time to collect his monthly checks.

Bobby considered Archer's hair remarkable when he first spotted him. It was long and lush, with a touch of frost. He had a clipped beard and crow's feet under his eyes, likely from reading late at night without adequate light. Bobby reckoned the old bloke was in his seventies based on the weathered and chiseled appearance of his face. As frequently evidenced by his tattered and worn attire, he often threw off a melancholy air as though he were succumbing to consumption and old age.

It was only a short time before Bobby took Archer on as his pet project. He wanted to give this man something to live for, at least make his last days on earth tolerable. Bobby did not feel sorry for the man because he would not want him to. When they first met all those years ago, Archer flashed Bobby a smile with significant wattage. It transformed his face, and the years dropped away from his appearance. Archer's eyes shone bright, some form of green, and his teeth gleamed like piano keys. If his voice wavered at all, Bobby knew it was because he hadn't spoken much in a while.

Remembering these times brought Bobby a warm smile, followed by a scream from deep within that forced its way into his mouth. He kept his grip on it and pushed it away. Anger had taken over, and he didn't want anyone in his life since it would mean having to put his confidence in them.

Choosing the path he needed to follow would be safer and easier. His fists clenched, and his teeth locked up once the would-be scream dissipated. He told himself to walk away for a while, to view this 'elephant' from a few miles away until he figured it out.

"Well, are you one of them or not?" Archer challenged. This snapped Bobby from his profound thoughts and back to the current situation. He looked over at Archer, unsure what to anticipate, but found his closest friend, thin and pale, sitting next to him.

"Of course, I'm not one of them. I am Bobby, your best friend. Do you want to stay at your house or mine while you heal?"

"I think we will be safer at yours. And, by the way, I know who you are, Bobby. I was testing to make sure," Archer replied with a wide-open grin and a pat on the shoulder.

Chapter 14

"Vampires!" Vicki exclaimed almost too loudly. She immediately covered her mouth to keep a snicker from escaping. "Luca quit. What the heck is going on over there?"

Luca took a deep breath and focused sternly on Vicki. "I'm not kidding around. The woman is Jade Holmes, and her community name is Lamia. She is an elder in the House of Alethia. Since she's gone through the awakening process herself, she is recognized as a leader because of her age, depth of knowledge, and inspiration to many fledglings going through the awakening process."

Vicki stared at Luca, trying to decide if he was serious or if this was merely an extension of the joke. She decided to play along.

"What is a community name?"

"The individual is given this name—you know what, we'd better finish shopping and return to this somewhere more secure and isolated later. I could get in a lot of trouble talking to you about this stuff." Luca grumbled. He took a deep breath and peered around the store to check if they were being observed. Even though she was baffled by his tone, Vicki understood the message. She thought he might be taking the joke a little too far.

Sunday traffic was light, and Luca took US 1 Southward and headed toward South Miami, turning right on Bird Road until he arrived at Sunview Estates. Just like other South Miami communities, his had its share of delightful and unpleasant properties. Local convenience stores with bars on their windows and few spots left for graffiti artists to paint stood as evidence that this one was beyond its prime. Luca resided in a duplex where construction took place many years before his birth, and the neighborhood had forfeited all hope shortly after that.

Vicki brought up the subject of the woman in the shop after dinner. Luca explained that certain people are predisposed to or even born with tendencies toward vampirism due to their genetic makeup. A natural desire presents itself later in life, generally around puberty, and causes difficulty in everyday functioning for the individual.

"For some, the manifestation may never occur; nevertheless, for those in which it does, the longer they go without satisfying this urge, the weaker they become," Luca explained.

"What do you mean by weak? Weak physically or emotionally?" Vicki probed.

"They usually develop a host of physical and emotional symptoms that only feeding can soothe," Luca observed Vicki to ensure she did not go into overload. He continued, "So vampirism is both a state of being and a life path. A vampire soul must awaken to the life that awaits them, and everyone finds their unique timeline for awakening and skill development. Some know their energy needs early in life, and some later. Ms. Holmes, as an elder, stays involved in these communities and can assist those suffering with their awakening and needs."

"Why does she have a community name?" Vicki asked again.

"A community name is a name a person chooses to be called after awakening. Each member of the coven chooses a phrase or expression that serves as their community name, and it typically discloses something about their character. For example, Ms. Holmes chose Lamia, and historically speaking, Lamia is considered a monster who kidnaps and later disembowels children. Along with the meaning 'big shark', which perfectly describes her character, Lamia's Latin interpretation is 'vampire', and the Arabic definition is 'fiend'. Take your pick. We must keep our distance from her since she isn't a nice person."

"So she's one of the living dead. How did we manage to see her during daylight hours?" Vicki asked, raising an eyebrow. "I assumed they only came out at night and that feeding meant they had to consume the blood of other humans. Is she a serial killer?" Vicki's curiosity kicked into high gear, her legs tucked under her rear as she leaned forward as if expecting a thrilling revelation. Her intellect was determined to uncover the truth, even though she half believed Luca. But her brain was stubbornly clinging to the vampire stereotype ingrained in her for as long as she could remember.

"Oh, how silly of me," Luca conceded. "Vampires, of course, are the undead that prowl the streets at night in search of human blood to drink, yet we encountered Lamia during the day when she should have been resting in her coffin. Perhaps you have a point." Luca excused himself and went into the kitchen to refresh his drink.

It surprised Vicki when she detected a dramatic shift in his manner, so she went to investigate. As quickly as the difference was noticed, it disappeared. The change was beyond her grasp, like reaching desperately for a runaway balloon; the string dangling so frustratingly close but the wind forcing it away, to be adrift forever.

Luca heard Vicki's footsteps approaching, causing a mix of emotions to surge. He turned to face away from her, his back deliberately positioned as a barrier. The muscle at the corner of his right eye twitched involuntarily, betraying the intensity of his inner turmoil. His mouth contorted into a grimace, reflecting his discomfort.

With arms tightly folded over his chest, Luca felt a surge of frustration and disappointment. He was a person who valued honesty, but only a select few were granted access to the vulnerable truths that resided within him. He had trusted Vicki with a revelation, only to be met with what seemed like laughter and mockery. That sense of betrayal gnawed at his core.

As he stood there, his silence spoke volumes. It was clear that Luca was hurt and angry. For now, he needed time to process his feelings and decide how to address this breach of trust. Vicki realized she had angered Luca when he didn't turn around. She stood there biting her lip until it started bleeding.

"Luca, I'm sorry. I misunderstood. Not every day a girl hears about vampires, you know." Vicki stood behind him, her lips slightly swollen.

Luca turned around, and they stared at each other for what seemed like hours but were only seconds. "There's one more thing," Vicki's voice was softer now, less confident. A gentle blush of pink on her cheeks made her look vulnerable, and Luca barely inhaled as she leaned up on the tips of her toes and tentatively pressed her soft lips to his.

Luca's head went misty, and his body engaged at the sensation of her lips, and then he tasted the blood. Just as he almost lost himself at that moment, Vicki retreated, an expression of embarrassment on her face.

"Luca, I love you," she pronounced as she wiped the blood from her mouth.

Chapter 15

"Wow! Is he for real?" Landers quizzed Mansfield as he entered the observation room door.

"Yeah, he is inconsistent in every way. In your research, did you find anything about medication or drugs he might be taking?" Mansfield questioned.

"No, not really. Why?"

"I'm with you, Dave," Slater intervened. "Something is wrong with him. He's speaking too fast and acting like his mind is spinning because he constantly wants to change the subject. Also, what's with the claim he doesn't need to sleep till he passes out?"

"Well, he responds, he just doesn't answer the questions," Landers inserted.

"It's because what he says is not truth in its entirety," Slater added.

It was still early, and the sun's climb was far from done. "I think he's a lot smarter than he lets on. Nevertheless, I have a sneaking suspicion that this man is either covering something up or suffering from a borderline personality disorder, and he isn't doing an excellent job of concealing it." Mansfield stopped pacing around the matchbox room, leaned into the window, and stared at Moody.

"Landers, go to the flat while he is here and call me if you find anything interesting. Check for medications and drugs, and search for traces of someone else living under the same roof. Don't ask why. I have a hunch. Slater, tell Sandra about an hour until official confirmation of the bodies, then you can go with me to take him to the crime scene."

Mansfield waited another 10 minutes before returning to the interview room. In case the issue of divorce came up, he carried the file from Evie's office with him. Once he entered the room, he sat down and started arranging his files and making notes on his paper pad without addressing the potential person of interest. Mark sat still, rubbing his chin and the back of his neck, waiting for the man to speak.

Once prepared, Mansfield looked up, pretending to be in deep thought, and asked, "How did you get along with your wife? I mean, I understand what you said about marriage and relationships, but how did you manage? Did much fighting go on?"

Surprised by the question, Moody answered, "Of course, we don't fight. We are not barbarians. Our children would never consider their parents exchanging blows. Disagreements of opinion are normal, like how to punish one of the children for an ill-advised action, but that would be the extent of it. It doesn't matter, in any case. Evie always wins. Arguing with her is like dueling with hand grenades."

"I understand," Mansfield encouraged and shook his head with approval. "Tell me about the last time you saw your kids and wife."

Moody started talking right away. "It was two days before I left for Austria. Evie knew I would be leaving the country and would be gone for a while, so she decided a family meal to discuss some matters before I left was appropriate. These are seldom lovely events. The four of us sat down at the table for pizza and salad, compliments of the pizza delivery service."

"Evie explained that she received another letter from Victoria's high school with an update on her grades and absences, and once again, they threatened to expel her from school if she didn't behave better. Of course, I supported her mother on this topic because Victoria needed to finish high school at least."

"Even though the conversation was tense, we managed to retain our composure and make a compelling case for the importance of at least completing high school. Evie's mention of Luca sparked my interest, but that's when the mother-daughter insults started flying. They cannot be in the same room for an extended period."

Mansfield interrupted, "Who is Luca?"

"Luca Medina is the 22-year-old Victoria met online. This was the first time I heard about it. I tried to bring down the temperature in the room, but the girls were in another dimension. Cooper and I tried to stay neutral."

Then, suddenly, the conversation turned to Victoria forgetting to pick Cooper up after his soccer game a few days earlier. I glanced over at Cooper, and he just shrugged his shoulders, saying, "No big deal."

"Next, Evie stood and banged her fist on the dining room table and yelled at Victoria, saying something about vaccines for stupid people. I needed to say something about that time. I couldn't let her talk to our daughter in that manner. But my strong-headed daughter stood and stared at her mother and said, 'Well, you could have taken him home yourself if you weren't banging his principal at the time!' My mouth dropped open, and I looked over at Cooper, shocked, and again he disavowed all.

"I glanced back at Evie, about to say something. I'm not sure what, but she interrupted by shouting back at Victoria and telling her that she should stop acting like she knew everything unless her name was Google. Then Evie stomped out of the room toward the kitchen, and Victoria ran toward the stairs. Cooper and I stood in the dining room and stared at each other. I kissed him on the cheek and left the house."

Mansfield stifled a laugh. However, he had absolute faith in Moody's story. The detective watched for the typical signs of lying. Still, instead, Moody held the right amount of eye contact, maintained steady breathing, blinking, and voice patterns, and spoke in complete sentences. Despite his hands and arms being animated, he never touched his face or throat, two frequent indicators of misdirection.

"Mark, do you own a shotgun?" Mansfield asked.

"Wh-what? Are you kidding? I was in Austria when this awful thing happened to my family. Am I under suspicion? Do I need a lawyer?" Moody became incredulous.

"I only ask to determine if the assailant brought the weapon with him or if he got it at the house. If the gun were already at the house, one avenue of investigation would be closed. This can cause a difference in which way we take the case."

"Oh. No, I do not own a shotgun," Mark replied, more at ease.

Mansfield decided not to address the divorce. He wanted to save that for another time. Since Moody left right after the outrageous dinner, it was reasonable to assume he did not know about it before he left the country.

Mansfield and Moody traveled to the coroner's office, close to Jackson Memorial Hospital, to identify the bodies of the three victims. Rita Slater arrived earlier and prepared a room for Mark. A soft glow from a muted lamp streamed, casting a warm ambiance across the space. The room exuded a sense of tranquility, carefully crafted by Rita's meticulous preparations. The air carried a subtle hint of lavender, courtesy of the scented candles artfully arranged on a small side table.

When Mark stepped inside, the door closed with a gentle click, enveloping the room in a cocoon of serenity. The walls, painted in a soothing shade of pale blue, offered a sense of calm and peace. Soft, plush armchairs were positioned near the window, inviting Mark to relax and bask in the gentle breeze that wafted through the slightly ajar glass pane.

An intercom in the room played some faint melodic tune, barely audible but soothing to the ears. In an effort not to upset families, no religious iconography (crosses, etc.) appeared anywhere in the room.

"Mark," Mansfield said, "a mortuary assistant, Ron, is on the way to explain the procedure. Attestation must take place through photographs of each deceased person. You do not have to rush to look over the photos. You can take as much time as you need. If needed, Ron might also offer to direct you to grief counseling or other services. I suggest you utilize these services."

As Mansfield finished up, the middle-aged morgue keeper entered the room, and Mansfield and Slater moved to the back corner, sat in the available chairs, and attempted to become invisible. The keeper walked Moody through the procedures.

"In conclusion," Ron said, "the photographs only include areas necessary for identification and, where feasible, avoid showing graphic injuries. We are here to make this process as non-traumatic as possible."

With that, Ron laid five pictures in front of Moody, face down, then stepped back and stood next to Mansfield and Slater. Moody watched the clock for a minute or two before he moved. At length, he reached up and turned the complete collection of photos face up and straightened the assortment so it was in perfect order.

The first picture was of his son, Cooper. He was lying on a metal gurney wrapped in some white cloth. A small but adequate cushion supported Cooper's head as he rested with his arms folded over his chest. Everything from his neck to his toes stayed covered.

Cooper's discoloration on his right forearm drew Moody's immediate attention. When he was six, he broke his arm after falling on the playground. Six weeks later, the doctors found the top of a ballpoint pen he'd used to scratch his itching. Undoubtedly, the cap had come off and been buried in the skin. Moody touched the spot, and a slight smile skirted across his lips. *What a knucklehead move.* The second photo showed a close-up of the fading blemish. Yes. This was his son.

One second, two, and three seconds passed—guilt seized Moody's heart, its grip tightening with each passing moment. An all-consuming fire ravaged his mind and clawed at his throat, leaving a bitter taste of regret. Waves of remorse crashed over him, uninvited and merciless, as he confronted the painful truth.

Love for his son surged within him, a potent mix of longing and sorrow. In the depths of his soul, he acknowledged the missed opportunities, the absent presence at sporting activities that his son held dear. Every missed game, every unshared victory or defeat, weighed heavily on his conscience. The ball that remained unkicked, a symbol of the emotional distance that had grown between them, haunted his thoughts. Moody stood at the precipice of his emotions, aching for redemption that he knew would forever elude his grasp.

The following print was Victoria, lying on her side facing the opposite wall on the same type of stretcher. Moody could only see the back of her head, hair, and left ear and shoulder. He could not see her face. The rest of her body stayed concealed except for her left leg and ankle. They lay draped on top of the white fabric, which concealed her body from the shoulder down.

Again, a disfigurement she received in the gymnastics class she took at the age of nine. Victoria practiced tumbling and landing into a pit of foam, where she got bitten by a brown recluse spider. This spider possessed a bite containing venom designed to immobilize prey, triggering a response in Victoria that was hard to ignore.

The bite, a tiny puncture wound, soon became a hotbed of inflammation and pain. It took a day for the venom to create a large blister and start spreading. The physicians cleansed the ulcer and removed enough of the affected region to guarantee the poison had been removed, but the healing process was lengthy, and an unsightly scar remained.

Over the years, the mark faded a little, but not much. As with Cooper, the following picture gave a closer view of the lesion. Yes. This was his daughter. His beautiful, intelligent, and witty daughter.

This memory did not feel good. The guilt now felt like gasoline in Moody's guts. His insides were dying of the toxicity, and he needed no more than a spark to set him ablaze. For him, there remained nothing but an outline of his former self.

The last photo in the pile was Evie. The presentation used a bed clad in white fabric. Like Cooper, Evie was on her back with her head on a small pillow. Moody stared at her face and the top of her shoulders. For the first time in a long time, he could look at her face without the heavy make-up she wore, as a rule.

Moody recalled how beautiful she was. The woman he fell in love with and married a lifetime ago rested before him. Regrets, he had so many regrets. *Where had she been these past several years?*

Moody let out an inaudible sigh. His mind was awash in recollections, like he was adrift in a vast ocean. He then turned around and spoke to the three witnesses waiting behind him. "Yes, this is my family. Thank you for allowing me to say goodbye." The attendant collected the pictures, and Mansfield and Slater escorted Moody out of the building.

"Mark, if it is not too much trouble, we would like you to drop by the house, take a quick look around, and then give feedback if you see anything that is amiss. As it is, we cannot ascertain if a burglary has gone bad or something else. This would help with the direction of the case. While we are on the premises, you can retrieve any items you might need for a longer-term stay at your practice studio," Mansfield offered. Moody agreed to go to the house, though he wanted nothing from the place.

Mansfield now had two choices: the opportunity to go to the apartment and observe what Landers found or go with Slater to the house and watch Moody's reactions. He called Landers to get an update, and Landers indicated he was almost finished and would meet him back at the station after lunch.

Moody rode with Mansfield, and Slater followed in the police cruiser. Still designated as a crime scene when they arrived, the house gave the impression of a home stuck in a place like a wax statue. After unlocking the front door, Moody entered the hallway and detected the foul odor permeating the residence. The truth was like a sour flavor on his tongue. No sounds, music, or light broke the suffocating slumber that had descended over the gloomy interior. Rather than react, Moody's spirit twisted in on itself like a tormented serpent.

When Mark entered his office, he slowed down and took his time as he approached his desk, scanning the area before sitting down. When he noticed the open drawers and the missing files, he altogether ignored the chaos. He looked up and around the walls at his accumulation of steins. In an instant, he located three that had vanished, even down to the precise spot atop the shelf where they had been displayed. Mansfield made a mental note to study the images taken the night of the murders to establish whether the steins were there then.

Slater took the report and put a BOLO out on the missing steins. Moody opened a desk drawer and produced the purchase receipt for each stolen piece. The cops did not seize these documents. Mansfield thought through the timeline. *Were these steins what the burglar wanted? Why only take three? Why even go to the second floor?*

Mansfield rubbed his chin and walked around the office, wondering what caused the perp to enter this house and what took him upstairs. He soon realized his jaw was aching, and his mouth had an awful aftertaste. Breathing into the palm of his hand, he now worried about bad breath. He did not want to be that police officer. More mints. He needed more mints.

Moody walked around the rest of the downstairs, noting nothing of significance. When it was time to go where the bedrooms were, he hesitated, gathering his reserves. He went straight to the main bedroom, being sure to avoid the roped-off areas, and sat on the bed to escape the detectives. He bowed his head in resignation, as if he were a withering flower, and tried to wipe the tears from his eyes. He gathered a few belongings and exited the house swiftly.

Chapter 16

"The refrigerator contains fresh fruits and vegetables, milk, and perishables. I thought that was odd for someone who knew they would be out of town for an extended period," Landers offered. "The place is properly junked up and appears to be lived in, nothing like the Angel Bluff house. No minimalist tendencies in this place. Neither the bathroom nor the nightstand by the king-sized bed contains medications."

"What was the temperature like?" Mansfield asked.

"Comfortable. Despite the chilly weather, the thermostat is set at 74 degrees, guaranteeing a comfortable indoor temperature. I find this ridiculous if he knew he was leaving for a few weeks or more."

"No pets of any kind?"

"Nope. I checked out the bathroom, and there were no signs of female products or a female touch. I checked the drawers in the dressers and the closet, and everything is more metrosexual if you know what I mean."

After lunch, Landers met Mansfield at the station to give him the full report. Moody's second home was a posh two-bedroom condominium in the South of Fifth neighborhood. The bungalows at The Yacht Club in Miami Beach came in all sizes, primarily large, with stunning views of Biscayne Bay.

What was initially designed as the family/dining room now contained a baby grand piano and everything else a pianist needed to practice and create. Sheets of paper littered the floor. As a result, the second bedroom became a television or leisure room, making the property a one-bedroom dwelling.

"However, two unusual things did pop up. It looks like an expensive pair of men's shoes was mistakenly left in the wardrobe. The issue is the loafers are somewhat smaller," Landers hesitated at this news.

"Maybe he received them as a gift, or he accidentally purchased the wrong size and has not returned them yet," Mansfield said as he examined the expression on Landers' face. "Is the footwear worn or new?"

"If you would listen, that is what I'm trying to say. They are well-worn." Landers stood waiting for Mansfield to understand. But the room stood silent. Mansfield wanted to smoke badly, but these government buildings didn't allow smoking. He missed the old days.

"Damn, Landers, I hate it when you find shit like that; it's distressing. What else did you notice as being strange?"

"On the side of the refrigerator, I found a magnet for the Miami Gun Club. I called the phone number, and they said membership for Mark Moody was not in their systems. Without a membership, the magnet felt odd unless he kept it because of the attached calendar."

"To put this case together, we must first eliminate a few loose ends," Mansfield started. "To begin with, it's evident Moody isn't telling us the full story. We must also consider Victoria's boyfriend, Luca Medina, to discover what happened with that connection. Then we need to discover Evie Moody's lover. Kisha from Trendsetters said she thought Evie's most recent lover was somehow connected to Cooper."

Mansfield stood, stretched his back, and stuck a toothpick in his mouth out of habit. He removed it immediately because his jaw and tooth socket had been bothering him recently. After mumbling, he threw the toothpick in the trashcan and picked up his jacket.

"Come on, Landers, let's go to the middle school and check out this principal. You looked him up before I arrived, didn't you?" Mansfield asked on his way out the door.

"Yep. His name is Lee Mendoza, and he is married with no kids. Been employed as a principal for four years with a clean sheet. This is all I could pull, given the time," Landers yelled while trying to catch up to Mansfield.

Once the detectives arrived at Cooper's Middle School, they learned the whole student body was attending a special assembly in his honor. Lee Mendoza led the gathering and would be back when the effort concluded.

Mansfield glanced around the principal's office and studied the photos of the family. "Not a bad-looking wife."

"You got that right. I don't believe I'd be stepping out if she waited for me to come home every night. Of course, he's not much. Cute dog, though."

The detectives took seats in the office and waited. "Do you remember your first trip to the principal's office?" Mansfield asked Landers.

"Sure do," Landers replied with a big grin. "The class was going on a field trip, and I forgot to get my permission slip signed. So, like any red-blooded American boy, I forged the signature. The problem I ran into was that I signed it, Mom." Mansfield and Landers both burst out laughing.

"You, dumb ass," Mansfield got out between bouts of laughter.

"How about you?" Landers asked.

"I told the nurse I was sick one day and had to go home. She couldn't find anything wrong with me, but I insisted on going home, so she sent me to the principal's office. They called my dad to come, and he insisted I tell him, right there in the office, why I had to leave."

"And then…"

"I had to go home because I had to fart, and I didn't want to do it in front of anyone. Everyone had a great laugh, and he told me to go to the bathroom and said that was where you went to fart, not home." There was another outburst of laughter from the two grown men, remembering their early school years.

A slender woman with a small-breasted figure gracefully entered the room and sat behind the desk. A pleasant fragrance trailed her. Her face was sad but lovely with intelligence. She had pulled her hair into a high, loose bun with stragglers falling around her face.

Mansfield and Landers recognized her as the woman in the pictures. She sat and waited as the men processed what was before them. Mansfield's attention was drawn to the reading spectacles perched on the crown of her head. Landers focused on the pictures behind the desk.

Finally, Principal Mendoza broke the silence with, "Hello, detectives. Sorry to keep you waiting. I understand you are here to discuss Cooper Moody."

Mansfield was the first to recover. "Uh… Yes. We are investigating the case and wanted to ask a few questions about Cooper and how he was doing at school. How did the assembly go?" Mansfield asked, stalling for time so Landers could get up to speed.

"Well, death requires school leaders to act with compassion, care, and awareness. We try to model for young people how to grieve. Fewer examples of servant leadership are better." Mendoza took a deep breath and settled back in her chair.

"A school becomes a place for storytelling and remembering. Classrooms, hallways, and even my office have become places to listen, share, laugh, and cry. My job is to help the student body through this tragic time."

"Can you tell me a little about Cooper?" Mansfield asked.

"Cooper was a scholar and an athlete. He never had problems with his teachers; they loved him and wished they had a room full of students like him. He was always on the Principal's list for academic achievement. His coaches all said he was very coachable and eager to learn. He went out for everything. He liked winning," the principal offered.

"Did he ride the bus, walk, or did someone pick him up from school?" Landers joined after he shuffled through the file sitting on his lap. He knew his partner would never let him live this one down.

"Most of the time, he had something going on after school, practice, a social event, or whatever. From what I've heard, his sister picked him up from school or activity after he finished his day."

"How well did you know Cooper's mother?" Mansfield asked.

Lee Mendoza only seemed momentarily surprised at the question but quickly recovered. Once she had removed her glasses from her head, she leaned forward and put her clasped hands in the center of the desk.

"How well did I know Cooper's mother?"

"Well, I want to be honest, but I don't want to speak ill of the dead," Mendoza paused and bit her lower lip. "Ms. Moody was a ghost parent. This is the type of parent whose name is on the roster, but educators are unsure if they exist. She's never been seen by Cooper's teachers and has never taken an opportunity to chat by phone or at parent's night."

"I understand, but you did not answer the question. Detective Mansfield asked how well you knew Evie Moody firsthand," Landers interjected.

"Oh, I needed clarification on the question. I'm sorry. Well, I have met the woman occasionally. She seemed nice. I have run into her at social events and fundraisers. She had a certain charm and came off as someone seasoned at forming business contacts through informal social meetings." Mendoza conceded.

"Still, I think she put personal relationships, like her family, below those that could make her money."

"What type of social events did you and Ms. Moody have in common?" the detective asked.

"My husband is in real estate, and so is she. I accompany him to events at times."

"We have information that you and Ms. Moody have been having an affair," Mansfield declared as he stared at the principal, giving her no opportunity to retreat.

"Am I a suspect? Do I need to call my lawyer?" She snapped in self-defense, and her posture became notably erect to signify she was dominant, authoritative, and in control of the situation.

"I don't know, are you? Should you? Do you have an alibi for the evening of October 19 between 10:00 and 10:30 pm?" Mansfield snapped back without blinking or changing an octave in his voice.

"I was home sleeping," she barked.

"Good. Can anyone verify that?" Mansfield said in an accusatory manner.

"My husband should be able to. He was out, but I was in bed when he got home. He would have activated the system, so the alarm company should show the times."

"Excellent. I would appreciate your cooperation if you could get this report from your security company for the entire month and drop it off within the next day or so. We need to ask for his alibi as well. This allows us to deal with both situations simultaneously. Shall we stop by your house tonight, or would you like him to stop by the station tomorrow morning?" Landers asked.

"That's up to you. I don't care," and with that declaration, Lee Mendoza left the office without hesitation.

Dave looked over at Mike. "You didn't know we were coming to see a woman?" he asked with one eyebrow raised.

"I… I never actually looked at the picture on the driver's license. I mainly skimmed over the details on the rap sheet."

Chapter 17

Poisonous repercussions await those who succumb to the darkness. Until Beverly DeMeglio became old enough to move into the college dorms, she observed her mother's spiral into oblivion. When her mother was desperate to go to the other side, she killed herself with one of her prescriptions. Beverly discovered her too late and phoned 911.

Beverly needed to talk to someone about her remorse and rejection because of the incident. She knew numerous people, but she only confided in two of them, and both were on buses to their out-of-state colleges. She should have appealed to her father, but she tended to see him as the source of the problem. A deep resentment for him began to fester.

After the officials removed her mother's body, her father said, "I want you to think more about how you influenced your mother's actions. You decided to attend college. That's why I thought she was so upset. Rather than being so self-centered, you could have exercised better judgment."

Beverly bolted for her room, slamming the door behind her. She hurled the bag she was packing across the room and collapsed on her bed, her head buried in her pillow. She had no idea what would take place next.

As a child, Beverly filled her world with silence. The air hung heavy with the anticipation of her father's absence, and she clung to the belief that if she remained utterly quiet, he would forget about her. It was a strategy she had devised, a desperate attempt to shield herself from the storm of her parents' turbulent relationship.

Unfortunately, this self-imposed isolation only served to amplify the ugliness that seeped into their home. Beverly could hear the harsh exchanges between her parents, their voices laced with resentment and anger. Although she tried to drown out the sounds, the words pierced through the walls, invading her sanctuary.

Whenever she stole a glimpse of herself in the one mirror in the house, the reflection staring back at her was far from the hideous troll she believed herself to be. Instead, she saw a young girl with delicate features and a quiet, haunting beauty that mirrored her mother's.

Beverly had been trained in social graces, a skill instilled in her through countless lessons and admonishments. She knew the importance of maintaining a façade of compliance, never daring to talk back to adults. Avoiding confrontation became her unwavering shield. She grew older and realized that her father's cruelty stemmed from the darkness within him, a burden she couldn't fathom.

At 16, Beverly confessed to her mother that she liked Eloise, one of the students in the science class, a lot. Every boy in the school wanted to know Beverly, but none ever piqued her interest. Her mother warned her it was customary to feel this way sometimes, but she should keep her feelings to herself should she be rejected for them. Now that she was older and more mature, she wondered whether her mother had ever told her father about her sexual orientation and whether he had been angry.

As soon as the funeral concluded, Beverly started collecting her belongings again to leave. Even though courses had begun, she could still enroll because the drop/add period had not expired. Her father burst through her bedroom door, still dressed in funeral attire; she froze and gazed at him.

"Just, what in the hell do you think you're doing?" No response. Beverly stood, too stunned to react. "You think you can still go to the college your mother said you were going to? You're mistaken. Beverly, you're a woman born to cook, clean, and bear children. It's one thing to do well in high school when there's nothing but idiots to compete with, but if you take your game to the next level, it just makes you a pathetic joke. While I'm still alive, there won't be any DeMeglio jokes, so don't worry about that."

He slammed the door so hard when he left that a piece of wood behind one of the hinges split. Just another incident that would undoubtedly be her fault. Beverly sat at the foot of her bed, her eyes fixed on the crooked door, and wept. She thought about her mother and understood how appealing the notion of escaping this place had become. She considered how lovely it would be to live without external forces for the rest of your life. The sensation was alluring, and Beverly rocked herself to sleep with that idea going through her head.

"What the hell is wrong with you? Can't you do anything right?" Fin DeMeglio yelled from the kitchen to his daughter. She rushed from the bed, her funeral attire still on. Although she knew exactly who produced the commotion, she went outside to investigate.

"You understand I must report to work today. Where is my breakfast, and where is lunch? It was empty when I picked up my lunch bucket; there is no room for excuses!"

"I... I'm sorry, Father. I... didn't know. I mean, I didn't think..."

"You are correct. You did not think. During the past 18 years, your mother cared for you in every way possible, including wiping your nose and ass. You must fill in for her now that she's gone. Every day, you can bet your life. I go to work and eat breakfast before leaving the house, take lunch with me, and expect dinner when I get home. Who the hell do you think is responsible for that since your mother checked out?"

"I'm making your lunch now. If you can wait a few minutes before you leave." Fin marched off to the bathroom and, as usual, slammed the door. Beverly looked around and found things to throw together to make his lunch, and when he returned, she promised she would go to the store and purchase better items for tomorrow. He threw a 20 at the counter and grumbled out the front door.

At the kitchen table, Beverly remembered a chemistry lecture from her senior year of high school in which they addressed barium acetate. Beverly smiled to herself as she recalled the incident. She stole a small amount of the drug in a plastic bottle and hid it in her room in case her father became physically violent toward her or her mother, but she had forgotten it until today. Looking about her room, she pondered where she would have stashed the bottle. In her initial guess, she stared at the object in her peripheral vision. Beverly contemplated the breadth of her knowledge as she held the toxic chemical.

The young woman showered and changed her clothes. Her first stop was the public library, where she researched barium acetate, its applications, and its potential adverse effects. As expected, the substance is known to induce heart attacks and does not appear in a standard autopsy. The chemical can only be detected with specialized equipment. She formed a strategy.

After arriving home, Beverly looked around the entire house for hidden cash belonging to her mother. She knew her mom had some since she had always been willing to give Beverly extra help when she was short, and she made her daughter vow never to tell her father. A Crisco can held the treasure on the pantry's top shelf. It wasn't until she opened the container that she discovered the money and a positive pregnancy test. The girl sat for a minute, and everything fell into place. A tear ran down her cheek.

According to plan, Beverly prepared dinner by the time her father arrived home from work. He grunted and sat down to eat, yelling for her to show her face. She did not respond, and he dismissed her the minute he began eating. Not feeling well after a few bites, he stumbled into his bedroom and found a note. He could barely read it before he fell face-first on the bed.

FATHER, I AM LEAVING AND WON'T BE BACK. GET SOMEONE ELSE TO SHIT ON. I DO NOT DO BREAKFAST, LUNCH, OR DINNER. AND MOST OF ALL, I DO NOT DO BABIES!

When the authorities found the corpse, the table had been cleaned, the dishes washed and put away, and the note had vanished. Beverly DeMeglio disappeared without a trace and may never be found.

Chapter 18

When Lee Mendoza first saw Evie Moody, she was 36 years old. Life changed from that day forward. It was April 1999, and Lee and her husband traveled to Tampa to attend the American Real Estate Society's annual meeting on the western coast of Florida. The city is a popular destination for business conferences and events, attracting professionals from various industries to its vibrant culture and beaches.

During their stay, Lee and her husband chose to accommodate themselves at the convention hotel, the Hyatt Regency Westshore. Situated in the Westshore business district, the upscale hotel was renowned for its luxurious amenities and convenient location. The Regency offered a wide variety of services, catering to the needs and preferences of the guests as well as the convention goers. Among the notable features were two swimming pools and a top-notch fitness club.

Lee's husband, Jake, was a successful real estate agent. His expertise and impeccable service built a devoted following among his Miami clients. His knowledge of the Miami-Dade market and his commitment to providing exceptional customer service made him a sought-after professional in the real estate industry.

Earlier in the year, Lee and Jake had celebrated their tenth wedding anniversary. Once they passed the seven-year milestone, Lee thought it was cause for elation. She imagined the rest of her marriage would be uneventful. It didn't entirely turn out that way. Despite their best efforts as a couple (including date nights and couples counseling), they ended up drifting into the role of roommates.

Jake was upbeat, pleasant to be around, and forthright, to a point. He sent out vibes of confidence and a willingness to help people. As a successful businessperson, he was meticulous in his job and had an extensive network of contacts. He was always moving around since he was one of the most influential people in town, and his knowledge was his power source.

However, at the house, everything had settled into a familiar pattern. He refused to talk about anything potentially different and was furious if plans had to be changed. Lee had become weary of their daily routine. As a woman and a wife, she felt rejected and detached as the sexual dry periods that had come and gone over the years became longer and longer.

She had discovered she longed to frolic and enjoy life playfully. She yearned to play Monopoly or Trivial Pursuit, toss a Frisbee, blow bubbles, or ride the swings at the park. Or she might merely read ridiculous jokes and hilarious stories to her hubby. She was hoping a weekend in Tampa would loosen them up a little. She was not going to relive her days as Beverly.

The schedule had the black-tie reception and dinner on Friday evening. Lee opted for a timeless little black dress by selecting a silk version with subtle ornamentation. She added polish to her presentation with a pearl necklace, a diamond bracelet, and heels. Jake sported a classic tuxedo look, complete with black accessories. His pleated white button-down shirt and patent leather shoes made quite the ensemble.

The pair looked stunning as they entered the celebration, exuding confidence and elegance. Jake introduced Lee to some newer faces in the room but then, unexpectedly, vanished into the crowd, leaving her abandoned and uncertain. Standing alone, Lee struggled to find her place among the curious onlookers, her glamorous appearance prompting questions about her identity. With a mix of apprehension and curiosity, she scanned the room, searching for a familiar face or anyone else who might share her sense of disorientation.

The man wearing the dark gray suit taking his time perusing the artwork on the wall caught her eye, and she maneuvered over to speak with him. Mr. Gray Suit was, to put it mildly, difficult to communicate with. However, a bigger group of individuals had collected not far away. She and her new acquaintance crept into the circle to overhear the conversation and look for a way in.

Lee kept looking around, hoping to catch sight of her husband. This bore-fest was about to kill her. Without causing a disruption, she stepped away and hit the bar for another drink. She started the evening with white wine because it made her more talkative. But since she was alone, she opted for a Daiquiri, thinking this would help her keep her faculties under control.

After reviving her spirit with a new drink, she gazed toward the room's center, where a group of men had congregated to form what could only be described as a makeshift town square. She suspected one of the men facing away from her was her husband, the loud one joining the others in their complaining. Most of the individuals in Jake's life were pawns in a chess game, and when his moves did not work out, he would become angry and raucous.

The vast reception hall's double doors were beyond the town square. As Lee analyzed the tuxedo, she assumed it belonged to her husband. The doors flew open, and the most stunning woman Lee had ever seen strolled in. Her presence gave a powerful 'I'm in charge here' impression, which intrigued Lee.

This middle-aged senior member of the group had golden-brown hair that looked as soft as a spider web. She illustrated the brilliance of a floor-length black Chiara Boni gown with side rucking and gathered ruffle detailing without fault. The halter design called attention to her long slim neckline and perfect posture. The stride of her step and curl of her perfectly decorated lips shouted, "I am a woman!" to anyone in her path.

She took her time walking through the crowd, nodding, and shaking hands with other attendees, sizing up the room with each step. While Lee turned to observe her husband's response, the woman moved to the bar, stood beside her, and ordered a Gin Rickey. She spoke to Lee with a direct look and introduced herself.

"Hi. My name is Evie Moody. What do you have, a Daiquiri? Smart woman. You must stay on guard in a room full of vultures like this. How did you get dragged to this dreadful event?"

Lee looked back at this person who spoke with such confidence and returned her offered handshake with a smile and laughed, "Well, I'm a plus-one. My name is Lee, and my husband, Jake Mendoza, is over there enthralled with whatever the discussion is with those men," she pointed over to the town square folks.

"Ah, Jake Mendoza. I would have never thought you would be with a man like him," Evie answered, her eyes sparkling.

"Why do you say that?"

"Well, even though you've been married for quite some time, I think it's fair to say most people would describe him as a large, noisy man with a piercing glare and a metallic chuckle. A guy of rough substance. A man who never stops using his booming, trumpeting voice to declare his meager beginnings. He's kind of a bully of humility," Evie grinned.

"But you, you are just the opposite. You are someone who wants to break free and have fun. Break the shackles of adulthood and engage the world, to do all the things you have missed."

Lee blushed. *How could this woman be so intuitive? Is she reading my mind?* Lee let out a soft laugh and retreated a step, putting some space between them. Evie reached for her highball glass and patted Lee on the hand, encouraging her not to worry. The future had promise. Lee wanted to flit about like a dizzy moth. Evie left and joined the other people in the town square.

Jake looked over at Evie and dismissively smiled. "Like I was saying, I was hosting an open house at a vacant property with no running water or electricity. Early in the morning, while people were milling around, I overheard a woman shriek from the hall restroom. I can't believe she let her five-year-old use the toilet in the $1.2 million home, where he left a load any buffalo would be proud of, and the damn toilets did not work. Horrified, as she should have been, the mother and kid ran out. With gratitude, the neighbors lent us a bucket, which I filled with water and used to fill the tank and flush the toilet."

Everyone erupted in polite laughter.

"Oh, Jake, if you are not monopolizing the conversation claiming to know more about the situation or pronouncing your solutions are better than anybody else's, you are delighting us with your most charming stories. What would we do without you?" Evie smiled and held her glass at eye level as a toast to the man addressing his constituents.

The rest of the weekend remained non-eventful. Lee kept herself occupied by stealing glances at Evie and engaging in idle chatter whenever possible. She gave the experiences some thought on the ride home. Despite her maturity, something about Evie made her feel young again.

Lee remembered the best, most innocent parts of herself and all her parts that needed nothing more than love to be whole and healthy again. She realized that if she spent all eternity next to this woman, she might melt into peace and contentment. She believed they would be a perfect complement to each other. Yes, Lee was well and, without question, smitten.

Jake kept his focus ahead, his face compressed, his lips flat, and his teeth clenched. Occasionally, he'd let out a soft growl or throaty sound. Before he finished, Lee glanced over and observed him murmur something. She couldn't tell what he was saying even though she saw his lips moving.

"What honey?" Lee asked in her 'Everything is wonderful' voice.

"Are you writing a book? You sure seemed to enjoy yourself this weekend," Jake responded with a scorn-filled half-laugh. Lee was insulted by the remark.

"You didn't? I thought the whole reason for going was to relax and enjoy ourselves."

"Well, that's hard to do with that bitch Evie Moody sniffing after you all weekend and you lapping the attention up like a starved puppy."

"What in the hell are you talking about? I bet I didn't say 20 words to the woman, and I found her to be most pleasant. Although, since you speak of her, I can understand why she doesn't think much of you."

"What the… Who the hell does she think she is, talking about me? She's the one who stole the listing from me. She's the one who interferes with my deals and shows up at my open houses. Like I don't get enough of her on the job, now I must listen to my wife sing her praises. This is just too much!" Jake slammed his fists on the steering wheel.

Lee watched her husband throw a tantrum—such a grown-up reaction. She thought that jealousy had a way of making one act like a child.

"You know what, Jake? Now that I have my master's degree, I will work full-time. No teaching, however. I want to be a school principal. I'm going to get started on that tomorrow."

"My silence doesn't mean I agree with you. It's just that your level of idiocy has rendered me speechless."

Chapter 19

Two days had passed since Mansfield first started looking into the case. He didn't want to, but he and his partner returned to the station for the weekly Friday morning meeting with the sergeant. When Mansfield finished talking to Lee Mendoza, he felt depleted. The more he talked, the worse his mouth became. His tongue had become painful and swollen, and he noticed blood spots.

He saw nothing strange when he glanced in the mirror, but he sensed something must be wrong. The sensation of having his tongue slashed was intense. He detected sharp splinters protruding through the skin while running his fingers over the inside of his lower gum line. Pieces of a tooth or bone had formed at right angles to his other teeth.

He had become everyone's nightmare. The tooth hurt enough when the dentist pulled it out, but the pain now that the nerve had been exposed tripled. To keep his mouth shut seemed to be the only way to survive.

Mansfield took aspirin and some gauze from the first aid kit once he arrived at the station. After swallowing the tablets, he placed the gauze between his gums and tongue. Even though communication became more challenging, this helped him avoid the urge to attack someone. When the detectives entered Morgan Johns' office, Mansfield's agony had faded to a dull throb. She sat behind her desk, waiting for them.

"So what's up storm troopers? Got anything on the triple yet?" Both detectives took a seat before they began their update. Among the ranks, Sergeant Johns stood out for her diligence and ingenuity. She did not waste time and would often go right to the matter. She smiled and waited.

Mansfield started, "A burglary took place as well as the murders. Mark Moody is missing three valuable antique beer steins from his collection. We examined the crime scene photographs. The steins were also missing on the night of the murder. We're investigating the husband, digging into the three victims' backgrounds, and following up on leads related to the burglary."

"Mr. Moody is the prime suspect with a rock-solid alibi. This doesn't prove he isn't complicit; it only proves he didn't pull the trigger. He discovered Evie, his wife, may have been having an affair with another woman before he left to go on tour. Also, his wife was pursuing a divorce, but I don't think he knew it. Then we still need to check out Luca Medina, the daughter's boyfriend. He is a bit older and might be promising. He's up next."

"Why are you talking so funny?" Morgan asked.

Landers jumped in. "Due to dental problems, Dave had a tooth pulled, and the wound doesn't look to be healing very well."

"I see," Johns said, giving Mansfield the once over.

"Back to Moody: he keeps a separate residence under the guise of a place to practice. In any case, more examination revealed that the condominium is frequented by someone other than Moody. We are working on tracking this individual down. We still want to interview Moody's agent to hear how he reacted when he heard the news," Mansfield finished.

"At Cooper's school, we uncovered nothing more sinister than the likelihood that his mother's affair was with the principal. Next, we'll visit Victoria's academy, and hopefully, that will give us some leads on Luca Medina," Landers added.

"What about the burglary?"

"We ran down the car reported parked outside of the house, and as of now, that's a waiting game," Landers answered.

"So far, no leads have surfaced on the missing steins. They are now recorded as stolen property. We can only assume the puke on the stairs belonged to the thief. This makes me believe he was either not involved in the killings, or he was working with someone else and was unaware of the impending violence," Mansfield said with care.

"After collecting the vomit, we submitted the sample to the lab for DNA testing," Landers said. "Forensics guarantees a minimum 90-day backlog in examining things from crime scenes. To be as blunt as possible, we have hit a stalemate on that front, and it is now in your hands to do all you can to break the logjam."

"Let me feed this back to you," the sergeant said after deep breathing and screwing up her mouth while tapping her nails on the top of her desk. "So far, you've provided me with two potential suspects. The first is the spouse although he wasn't the killer. Since you think he may be involved in the murders, we must assume he hired or induced one of the perpetrators to carry out the homicides. Correct?" Landers sat still while Mansfield shook his head and glared at Johns.

"The second possibility presented to me is a burglar, and we know there's one since your primary suspect claims three antique steins are missing. We might utilize the biological evidence found on the steps at the murder site to identify this perpetrator, but doing so will take over 90 days, by which time the sample may be worthless. Do I understand what you are saying?" She watched her detectives, and they both nodded their heads in agreement. Morgan's furious rant was making Mansfield angrier by the minute.

"The fact that a parked car was in front of the home while the crimes occurred lends credence to either explanation. Still, that leads nowhere," Johns said, reeking of sarcasm.

"Well, let's play a little more of this murder mystery and go with Plan C. Maybe Moody hired the burglar to steal the steins and kill his family." Morgan Johns shifted her weight in her chair from one side to the other. Each detective sat still and waited for Johns' lowered brow, thinned lips, and flared nostrils to dissipate. They referred to this as her 'angry face'. They knew better than to talk when it appeared.

After waiting a reasonable amount of time, Mansfield offered, "Morgan, Yes, I agree with you. Moody is the primary for now. He could have paid someone to kill his family and steal the antiques on the way out. I realize a thief did not decide to break into the residence and wreak all this mayhem without reason. However, a burglar may have broken in before the murderer did and hid when the killer arrived at the house. Assuming this is true, the fact that a murderer and a thief both showed up at the same house on the same night is indeed a coincidence."

"Do you believe in these types of coincidences?" Johns inquired.

"No. Not really. We are just two days into a triple homicide investigation, Sergeant, so I realize this isn't the update you wanted. We still need to explore many potential avenues of inquiry. Moody's male companion should still be located, as should his agent, the daughter's boyfriend, and the steins and automobile. Many loose ends still need to be nailed down," Landers summarized.

"I get it. I wouldn't say I like it, but I understand. Mansfield, fix that tooth, and let's wrap up this investigation. Many people are interested in this case, but we can't disclose that our leading suspect was in Austria at the time of the killings. They would laugh us out of town," Johns closed her file, and the detectives bolted.

Chapter 20

Aside from technical details like the type of weapon used and data about the crime scene, little else was available about the investigation. For Bobby, this was like two edges of a blade. He interpreted this to mean the police had come no closer to finding the real killer or coming for him.

"Why do you always watch the news channels?" Archer wondered.

"For the simple reason that we want updates on the investigation status," Bobby answered for the one-hundredth time.

"Yes, you're right; the house is where they keep the clones concealed as they develop them. One night, I spotted one of them leaving the building."

"Man, what are you talking about? When did you last visit Angel Bluff?" Bobby inquired, fishing to see what else Archer had to say.

"Sure, on a stormy night with lots of thunder and lightning. I got out of your car and walked into the yard of the toaster house to see what was going on, and someone came right out of the front door carrying what might have been a rifle, a shotgun, or just an umbrella. I turned to run, but he caught up and hit me on the head, which is why I am a target. They are convinced I witnessed something," Archer explained. Since the event, Bobby had yet to hear much from Archer.

"Why were you in my car?"

Archer stared at his friend and opened and closed his mouth several times before forming words. Lines formed between his eyebrows, and he tilted his head and asked, "Are you sure?"

"Am I sure of what?" Bobby responded, baffled.

"That I was in your car?"

"You just said you got out of my car," Bobby complained.

"Oh!"

Bobby threw up his hands and let out an exaggerated sigh. He walked to the kitchen and rubbed his brow to relieve a headache. He needed another drink. While standing at the counter, gathering himself, he caught sight of the loot pouch he used in the burglary, thrown in the corner. He stood still, holding his refreshed beverage, staring at the bag.

Bobby decided the sludge that had been passing through his brain these past few days must have decreased his oxygen intake and caused mental deterioration. What else could be the reason for the time slipping by?

Almost three days, it had been almost three days since the burglary. In all this time, no one had contacted him to give delivery instructions or the rest of the payment for his services. Stunned, he placed the fresh beverage down on the counter. He had been caught in the drama, and the whole reason for this mess sat before him. Bobby lowered his head and rubbed his eyes. When he glanced up at the pouch again, he screamed in frustration while backing away from the nook and knocking over a chair.

Archer ran into the kitchen, "Bobby, what's the matter? Are you okay?"

"Over in the corner!" The older man turned and saw nothing but the bag. He walked over and picked up the pouch.

"There is nothing over here except this small waterproof pouch," his friend said with reassurance. He held the pouch out for Bobby to take. Bobby moved away from the container, fearful. Archer watched him with caution and extended the bag again. Bobby took it and dropped it on the floor like a hot potato.

"What's in the package that has you all cranked up?"

"Don't you remember this pouch? We brought it from the toaster house," Bobby encouraged.

Archer picked up the sack, turned it over several times, and shook his head in the negative. "What's in it?"

"I don't know. We went there to get whatever is in it."

"You are right. I was the get-away driver," The older man smiled, acknowledging his ability to recall.

"Yes!" Bobby yelled and then grabbed his friend and gave him a huge hug. This nightmare could be over soon. "Do you remember why we went to the house?"

"Of course, I do," Archer said. "You needed to steal some papers from the owners of the house. You had a contract, and we wanted to prove that the aliens were creating clones because you knew where they kept the diagrams. You took too long, so I got out of the car to check on you, and that's when one of them came out of the front door."

"You are within reach now, oh so close, my friend. Can you describe the person who hit you?"

"He was average. It was so dark that I couldn't tell if he was Black, White, Hispanic, or what. He was wearing a long raincoat and was carrying a shotgun. That is what he walloped me with."

If Archer could lose the aliens, he would have a description and story to tell the authorities. Bobby grabbed the pouch and removed the manila envelope. Although the contract indicated the contents must be unopened for him to receive his final payment, it did not seem like anyone was coming to claim the goods. He ripped the pouch open and pulled out the contents. He and Archer both experienced the joy of Christmas morning.

The envelope contained several sheets of paper. The would-be burglars thought things of value, like diagrams, contracts, pictures, anything, would be in the package. Instead, they had 10 blank pages of writing paper. They searched through the pile several times, threw them down, and peered at each other.

Bobby spoke first, "WTF."

Chapter 21

Suflet Intunecat took his time opening his eyes. He saw tiny slivers of light shadow dance on twigs and leaves covering him; he tried moving cautiously. In taking an inventory of his body, he found his back tucked between something resembling rough tree bark.

The protruding roots and uneven surface were tormenting his ribs under him. Twigs snagged at his hair and scratched his face, and a spider web crisscrossed overhead. After knocking the spider web away, he rose to see he had tucked himself into a split area in a tree trunk for the night. It was as though his physique had aged 40 years at once.

After wiping the eye boogers from his face, he stood, stretched, and observed the area. The weather had become colder, but he was still alive. He licked his dried lips; his mouth tasted gritty and bitter. He listened and picked up the sound of water trickling to his right. The brook's beauty left him speechless. Is this the first time anyone has seen these things? He pondered.

A delicate balance existed in the water, robins-egg blue color, like the subtle sweep of a painter's brush. Trickling and snaking smoothly past all obstacles, the creek managed to leap over the strategically placed boulders. Twigs, serving as messengers from the mountain trees they had come from, twirled on the babbling surface.

The brook flowed over the pebbled riverbed and sounded like the airy, velvety whirl of a flock of birds. Beyond the stream, the mountains stood silently, a brooding presence of something more magnificent. Glinting and ingenious, a waterfall with a distant thrumming sound flowed down the mountain and fed the river. Suflet Intunecat bent down and scooped a hand through the water until he had drunk his fill. He found the wetness thirst-quenching.

He leaned against a rock and closed his eyes, enjoying the sun's warmth. The sweet perfume of the wonderful outdoors drifted to his nostrils as he reflected on the beauty of nature. When he was about to leave, he saw something shiny near a bush and had to turn around. It was a rusty, jagged blade stuck in some rotten wood.

One of the tarnished twisted bolts in the handle held the whole thing together. Suflet Intunecat eyed the knife like solid gold before stowing the rusty item under his prison-gray clothing. After making sure no one was watching, he headed out downstream.

The further he walked, the more Suflet Intunecat realized how hungry he had become, and he did not know how he would feed himself. He should have arrived at the cottage he'd spotted through the window by now, but instead, he was still determining how to get back in the right direction and was wandering. His departure from the castle of the infirmed was a baffling mix of incredible commitment and complete lack of forethought—not particularly strange for a 13-year-old.

Up ahead, he overheard what sounded like a child talking, and he halted abruptly. He moved silently and cautiously, breaking as few branches as possible, keeping the creek on his right. What he witnessed was nothing short of miraculous. The cottage he was trying to find appeared right before him. At least, he assumed it was the cabin, albeit the rear.

A small girl, about five years old, sat outside amid a circle of stones and logs, playing and singing with her dolly. Suflet Intunecat wanted to fly from the trees and give her an embrace. After meeting her, he was sure she would be his favorite.

He approached the child and spoke softly, "Hi. Can I play with you?"

The girl jumped at his voice, grabbed her doll, and clutched it closer to her chest. She did not scream, and she did not run. She just stood there looking at the boy with a strange expression.

"Why are you so dark? You in a fire or something?" she asked. Suflet Intunecat wrinkled up his face trying to understand what she was asking. She leaned forward and touched his arm. He looked down and understood.

"I don't know. I have always been this way. Can I play with you?"

"I guess so."

The two sat by the stones and wood, and she told him about her imaginary world full of ponies and princesses. Her older brother burst in while they played quietly and started yelling. He reached out and snatched his sister's arm, intending to yank her away. Suflet Intunecat grabbed her and began to drag her in the opposite direction.

"She is mine; you cannot have her," Suflet Intunecat snarled.

The little girl started crying and yelling for her mother. The door opened at the back of the cabin, and a healthy-sized woman appeared, shouting at the children to stop terrorizing each other. She stopped mid-sentence when she saw the Black stranger.

Scared by his mother's interruption, the boy let go of his sister, causing him to fall backward and hit his head on a large, sharp stone. Suflet Intunecat and the 50-pound child went flying in the other direction, and she landed on top of him and did not move. The mother ran down to where the children played and considered the blood leaving her son's brain in surges, beat out by a slowing heart. The mother went over to take her daughter from the interloper, but she did not move either. She stared into the eyes of the trespasser and witnessed nothing but a starving boy dressed in rags and freezing to death. She swooped in and grabbed her child, only to discover that her daughter's clothing contained blood splatter and the bloodied, jagged blade was in the teen's hands.

A phantom hand clamped over Suflet Intunecat's lips as he watched the lady clutch the children and cry frantically. A similarly spectral injection of adrenaline pierced his heart, immediately releasing its force. His rib cage heaved as though tied with cords as he fought to breathe. His head became a carousel of fears spinning out of control, each one pushing his mind into total blackness.

He tried to escape but was stuck in time and space. It seemed like he was no longer in the body, lying unmoving on the rough path, and adjacent noises were far away. He could hear other people rounding the house, shouting for their mother, and he intuitively knew that if caught, he would be sent back to the castle or be killed. He dropped the blade, which caused so much harm, scrambled to his feet, and darted back to the brook.

Suflet Intunecat discovered a cave with an underground passageway a few miles from the cabin. The tunnel curved coldly away into the eternal darkness, and the light shown on the walls at the tunnel's mouth diminished as it snaked away. He became emotionally and physically exhausted, and it was almost dark. Suflet Intunecat trembled. He lost focus, searching for a way out. He contemplated going back but did not comprehend how that would work.

Instead, he curled up, and before counting to 10, he fell asleep. Awakened during the night by a commotion outside the cave, two individuals inside the tube grabbed Suflet Intunecat. They dragged him farther in till he could no longer use his senses. He walked quite a distance, tripping over rocks and other things but eventually stopped at a set of ancient stone stairs.

Old torches provided light, and he could see the men who led him here shared dark skin like his. They told him people were looking for him for murder twice and that his darker skin made him an easy target. As soon as they received the news, they understood exactly where to locate him without delay. These men comprised part of the underground revolution to overthrow the communist rule in Romania. Suflet Intunecat told them as much of his story as he knew, and they promised to get him some education and transportation out of Romania.

Suflet Intunecat spent the following several years working with these people underneath the castle at night and managing the castle's upkeep during the day. As the master conducted several gatherings nightly, some days were more accessible than others. Seeing the far castle in the distance from his orphanage room, Suflet Intunecat quickly concluded that he was hiding under the great vampire's castle. The men training him assured him that, so long as he remained loyal and never met the master, the master would provide the opportunity for him to escape to America and have a long healthy life.

It took five years before the right opportunity occurred; however, in 1987, Charles Gray left Romania and established himself in America.

Chapter 22

On a Friday at 7:30 am, Mansfield was waiting for his dentist at his office. Dr. Williams arrived early because Mansfield called the office emergency line the night before, claiming something awful would happen, such as an extraterrestrial erupting from his mouth and taking over his body if he didn't do something fast to relieve the detective.

Mansfield's hand, clenched around the phone, shook in anger. This was among the worst tortures. Even though he was unable to cry or scream, he would occasionally incur lip trembling, which made him feel like a toddler. Not acceptable!

"Alex, something must give here. The wait is intolerable, and now I find it difficult to focus. No one should go through this," Dave Mansfield bellowed as best he could with gauze between his teeth and tongue.

"A normal filling turned into a root canal, which ended up with an extraction. There is decaying tooth debris in the void left by the missing molar; I guess that's what it is, and I'm experiencing this unbelievable aching. The damn pain radiates from one half of my head to the other and down my neck. Now, my throat feels flaming hot, and I can barely swallow. It's not getting better, and I must work! How in the hell can kids deal with this shit?"

"Dave, as I told you last night, a dry socket is where the underlying bone and nerves are exposed, resulting in suffering to the nerves radiating to the side of the face. We will pack the inflammation with medicine. Come back in a week if the throbbing persists, and we'll fill it up again, but you must cooperate. No drinking through straws and no smoking until the site heals. You will do nothing but continue to aggravate everything if you don't."

"Next week, my ass! Can't you make it stop now?"

"As for the sharp edges you are feeling, they are dead bone fragments that work themselves through the gums slowly as a natural healing procedure sometimes. We will grind those down, so they will no longer scrape your tongue. Hopefully, this will allow you to heal, and no more pieces will appear."

"Hopefully, what the hell, doc? Does every adult go through this?"

"No, only the stubborn ones like you. As I said, here are some antibiotics for you, but you should give your mouth at least another week to improve. I'll furnish you with more pain relievers, but I'm telling you, if you are not better within 14 days, you will have to go to an oral surgeon," Alex said.

"Gotcha. I understand. I have this horrible case I need to be able to solve while going through the process. I can't let this tooth thing stop me cold," Dave explained.

At the same time, Landers picked Rita up, and they arrived at Darryl Jenkins's office, Mark Moody's agent, the minute the doors opened. The police's interest in interviewing Mr. Jenkins caught him off guard. After quick introductions, Landers got right to the questions they were there to ask.

"Mr. Jenkins, we want to talk briefly about Mr. Moody's reactions when you let him know his house had been broken into and his family killed."

"Oh. He was asleep, and it took a while to wake him because he had been at the beer garden celebrating a superior performance. His first question related to how they died. I told him I did not know because the detective didn't tell me. He went into overdrive, shouting out instructions left and right. He wanted me to book his flights immediately and the remaining group home when reasonable."

"Once I got his itinerary, he wanted me to call the police back and give them the specifics because he was sure they would have someone to meet him in Miami when he landed," Darryl replied. "The rest of the day was routine, getting him packed and to the airport on time, making arrangements for everyone else. Not much talk at all about what happened."

"So nothing out of the ordinary occurred while in Austria?" Landers inquired.

"I would not say that. He started in a pissy mood until we got to Salzburg. The venue was magnificent, and this made him happy. He was going to spend an extra half a day in Salzburg before moving on to Vienna," Jenkins reflected.

"Also, when we could check out our accommodations in Salzburg, I found a global phone call on our account. I made a fuss about the cost with the clerk because we don't make universal calls from the hotels we stay in; they're too expensive. Company cell phones are international, so we use the minutes on our plan. Mark's room number had been entered as the bill-to-room because the call originated in the lobby. I tried to argue that anyone might put any room number in an automated system, but the call went to Miami, Florida. I thought those odds were a bit much."

"I understand. He was likely calling to obtain more information on his family. I'm sure. Do you still have the invoice?" Slater asked. Darryl went to a file cabinet, searched for a moment, and pulled out the bill. Rita asked if she could take a copy with her, and they left, thanking Darryl for his time.

Once in the car, Rita tore into the envelope and scoured the document, and there, in plain view, was the number in the States he dialed. "Bingo!" she exclaimed, excited they finally had a lead. When Mike and Rita appeared at the station, Mansfield parked his car. They could not wait to share the good news. Mansfield, in no agony now because of the Novocain injection he received earlier, was also happy with Landers and Slater's direction. Now they had to pull the thread and watch for what would unravel.

Landers jumped on the computer, hit a couple of keys to cross-reference the number, and waited while the software invaded the collective data of society. Mansfield was pacing. He reached for a cigarette and placed it between his lips, forgetting where he was and, more importantly, what the dentist had told him not more than an hour ago. Landers and Slater turned and stared at him as he fished his lighter out of his pocket.

Mansfield looked up as he started to light the cancer stick. "Oh shit," he said as he turned and threw the cig in the trash. "Anything yet?"

Landers looked down at the screen and almost choked. "You guys are not going to believe this. The number belongs to a Mr. Charles Gray who resides at, wait for it, wait—The Yacht Club—Miami Beach."

"Are you kidding?" Mansfield rushed to look at the screen himself. "Same unit number and everything?"

Slater observed the two men congratulating each other with high-fives and doing a little thank you dance behind the desk. "All right, you two, I give. What does this mean?" she asked.

"Oh, Slater, this is incredible. This is the apartment, a condominium, where Moody goes to practice to avoid being at Angel Bluff. This means someone else lives there with him. Some other male lives there."

Chapter 23

"The day I swallowed blood for the first time will forever be etched in my mind. I was around seven years old when I cut my finger and, like most kids my age, tried to stop the bleeding by putting the finger in my mouth. My favorite part was the flavor, which had a pleasant combination of saltiness and metallic undertones."

"Though many individuals had swallowed blood before and did not pay much attention, I found the flavor energizing and refreshing. My craving for the taste, smell, and rush of adrenaline drove me to hide in the closet and inflict minor wounds on myself over many days and weeks. I only needed insignificant amounts, so simple cuts and pinpricks were enough. The realization that I was unique started to set in when none of the other children did the same thing."

"I met another kid near the end of second grade and persuaded him to meet me behind the sports field, so we could try 'feeding' off each other's blood by making little wounds in our forearms. His distinctive flavor became fascinating to experience. He lost interest one day but said he would let me 'feed' off him in exchange for my lunch money. Not for long, however. At once, I realized this was only a band-aid fix."

"As I grew into my teenage years, I recognized I could explore the minds of other students in my classes. I made a game of these emphatic abilities by trying to guess what they would say. This mental energy created an unrestricted 'high', remarkably like blood feeding. My focus started to include the emotions of others, which turned into an explicit energy feed, different from the blood feed, but just as satisfying. It didn't take long for me to switch out my emphatic and emotional energy for the blood energy that had been so elusive and inconvenient. I started questioning if and how my identity as an instinctive predator may change things."

"Even though I don't consider myself a vampire, I researched as much as possible and watched every vampire movie available. The more research I did, the more I understood the film industry's attitude toward vampires centered around whatever made money, not the truth. As time went on, I realized the emphatic and blood energy that characterized my health would come to rule my existence. I am a true, modern-day vampire, and this energy level is part of my health."

Luca hoped this answered Vicki's question. He paused for a moment and waited for her reaction. She was lying on the sofa with her head in his lap as he talked. After silence filled the room, she got up and paced the floor, pinching the space between her eyes.

"So turns out you weren't trying to make me laugh all day. You mean this, in truth, exists?" Vicki probed. Luca nodded in agreement before resting his head in his palms, elbow on the sofa arm, and letting her take in what he had said.

"I'm sorry, but I just don't know what to say. I bet these were trying times for you, I imagine." Vickie stopped pacing, returned to the sofa, and sat beside Luca with her legs folded under her. "I guess I always had the impression that vampires exist, maybe not how you portray them, but surely in some form. They struck me as being more comparable to sociopaths, to be honest." Luca couldn't help himself, and they both exploded in laughter.

"This puts things in perspective. I've got a hundred questions," Vicki exclaimed. "First, what is your community name?"

Luca had to grin. He turned to face Vicki. "My name in the local community is Delano. It is a French word that translates to 'of the night'. Nonetheless, you can't call me Delano; it's inappropriate. This is a moniker only coven members are allowed to use."

"Uh-huh, what is the name of your coven?"

"I belong to the House of Nuit Rouge. As with my name, this one is also a French term with a crimson meaning. The term originates in New Orleans; the family history is intertwined with the Buffalo-based House of Alethia," Luca answered.

"Gotcha. Sign me up. How do I become part of the House of Nuit Rouge?"

Luca tensed. Here is the question he feared. This would be the end of the relationship. Is this what he needed to do to keep her safe? Should he tell her everything? He sat there and fretted as all the options and consequences flashed through his mind. In his experience, everything always appeared to turn out the same when he followed this path.

Vicki asked, "What's the matter? You seem troubled. Tell me what you are thinking."

"Vicki, you are not a vampire. At least, I don't think you are, and you have never indicated you might be. Therefore, you cannot be a member of the inner circle. Everyone we associate with in the center isn't a coven member. Many are unaware of the culture. Most of the coven's members aren't goths; they are professional people. If you didn't know any better, you wouldn't guess their cultural preferences based on meeting them."

"Oh," Vicki said detachedly. "So this is a major part of your life in which I cannot participate. You expect me to be fine with you holding clandestine gatherings, drinking the blood of unnamed people, and performing obscure rites dating back thousands of years? You want me to be a shell of a girlfriend. I should spend my time looking like myself but not let anyone else see everything beneath the skin is broken." Tears were swelling up in her eyes.

"No, Vicki, I don't want to do that. There are Black Swans in the House of Nuit Rouge. These are the kind of folks who provide their services to thirsty vampires. Most of the time, it is not about sex. They all use their unique approaches."

"For example, most of the Black Swans use a disposable scalpel to make tiny pricks on their bodies, and the coven member uses his fingers to squeeze the area until blood comes out. They will put their mouth right over the warm liquid and lap it up, repeating the process two or three times before cleaning and bandaging the wound," Luca explained.

Vicki interrupted, "Yuck. Why would anyone want to do that?"

"A person may decide to donate for several reasons. They have a close vampire friend who can relate to the situation, or they are motivated by the salary they receive. They do the job in exchange for sexual favors on occasion. Black Swans are accessible to everyone in the group and not just a select few, so working in this capacity is not a prestigious or desirable position. This is an undervalued but crucial part of our society's fabric."

"In our community, Black Swans are voluntary and paid very well. As I said, we came from New Orleans, an offshoot of the Buffalo population. They tend to perform things more genuinely and traditionally, close to how they were first taught in Romania." Vicki gave Luca a strange gaze indicating he should proceed with examples. "For example, and I'll only give you this one example, Black Swans are a mandatory part of their group dynamics and are often rescued enslaved people brought over from Romania. To be free is a reward earned by faithful, steadfast, and dedicated people."

"Let me tell you a true story. One time, not long ago, I went four months without feeding, and my previous girlfriend, Krystal, rushed me to the hospital. She had zero background knowledge on the subject. I went to the emergency room with a lowered heart rate that would shoot up to 150, sometimes 170, whenever I stood or walked around."

"A massive migraine followed this and a loss of consciousness. The doctors were undetermined. Then one day, I recovered, and they released me. One of my friends, a clan member, came to visit me and fed me what I needed," Luca replied.

Vicki sat on the sofa and stared at Luca. As unbelievable as all this was, she felt sorry for him and wanted to put her arms around him and tell him all would be fine.

"Back to the other thing you said about being unable to talk about the meeting and ancient rituals. I can come home and share this part of my life with you, but we must be incredibly careful. Like the rest of the world, the vampire lifestyle includes its criminal element."

"Most of these criminals are called slayers—deranged individuals who try to harm or kill people they suspect are vampires. They are psychopaths, sociopaths, or whatever label you want. Therefore, many of us do not advertise our affiliations. However, more than that, we, mixed couples like you and me, have Lamia to worry about," Luca agonized.

"She is in a completely different clique. What does she have to do with your group and with us?"

"Remember, I told you she was not a good person, and we needed to keep clear of her? Well, here is why. I don't know what you would call her. She is not a slayer but an internal police force or something close. Even though she is in Miami, she has strong ties to Buffalo and Romania. Whatever the case, she has made it her mission to keep an eye on everyone who isn't part of the Buffalo line to identify any potential slayers or plants from less hospitable nationally renowned covens."

"Our roots are in New Orleans, so she does not consider us friendly. Anyone who gets too close to a community without being part of the inner circle is on a monitoring list. I'll see if your name makes a list, and I can consider putting out the word that you have the protection and strength of the Dark Kiss. However, this is a double-edged sword. Doing this lets the slayers know you are important to a vampire, and you will become one of their targets. So whose list is worst to be on, Lamia's or a slayer's?" Luca concluded.

Vicki gave in, reached across the sofa, and hugged Luca with all her strength. She asked, "Does Hallmark make a 'Sorry, I tried to cut your arm, lap up your blood, and touch you in an ambiguous manner' card?" As he laughed, Luca spilled his soda all over the sofa.

"I love you, Vicki."

Chapter 24

Mansfield stood outside the exclusive Catholic high school where Victoria Moody studied. He witnessed a frantic rush from the overflowing parking lot as students sprinted to beat the bells ringing. Controlled chaos prevailed among a cacophony of noises. This species hadn't been exposed to the notion of personal space, so once Mansfield realized he'd left his pistol in the car, he felt a sense of relief.

The administrative building stood out as the single structure people avoided at all costs. As he arrived for his meeting with Principal Frank Dennison, the investigator introduced himself to the assistant monitoring traffic at the front of the property. She made a note and asked him to sit on the plastic chairs inside the doors made to fit a rump 30 years younger than his. She then talked into a communication device.

The educator in the adjacent room attempted to correct a disruptive teenager. According to the conversation, the classroom instructor allowed free speech on a touchy subject, and the student took issue with some statements being made. His comments set off a strong reaction from the teacher, and she ultimately lost control of the class.

This student's behavior became disruptive, and he had to go to the office for counseling on appropriate classroom conduct and instructor respect. When Mr. Dennison stepped up, Mansfield was shaking his head from a similar memory. An older woman, whom Mr. Dennison introduced as Ms. Walker and Victoria Moody's guidance counselor, waited in the office. He flashed his world-famous smile, showing off his perfectly straight teeth, and sat in the chair designated for him. This method was part of his plan to catch these intelligence sources off guard.

After introductions, Mansfield began, "Can you tell me a little about Victoria Moody?"

Ms. Walker responded first. "Ms. Moody studied with us for two and a half years. Her first two school years were fantastic, and she proved to be a brilliant student. She exhibited a growth mindset and became confident in her capacity to master new materials. Victoria believed the time and work she put into her studies would pay off. She had the confidence to try new things and the ability to think creatively. Always organized, consistent, and persistent."

"However, something happened over the summer; she came to school a different person this year," Ms. Walker fretted. "In our first meeting, to set our expectations as a junior, she told me to call her Vicki from now on, and she had trouble setting her goals. She claimed she had reached a point where she couldn't understand how what she learned in school applied to her daily experiences. To this day, I am at a loss to recognize her current state of mind and what caused her abrupt shift of perspective."

Mr. Dennison offered, "Victoria began hanging around with a different crowd and clothing herself more distinctively this year. It's not unheard of for someone her age to experiment with a new identity, but I got the impression she was trying on a character that was not a good match. Many teachers began to label her as a troublemaker."

"What do you mean, dressing differently? I'm certain I spotted unified attire among the group."

"Yes, of course. However, the females can wear the same uniform with an extreme individual twist," Ms. Walker interjected. The detective had difficulty understanding. "Some young ladies roll their skirts up at the waist, so the skirt is too short; others buy their shirts too small, to name a few things."

Mansfield nodded as a mental image formed. "What did she do to cause trouble?"

"Well, nothing so bad, really. Some teachers began not to like her. Not because she acted out in class; she didn't. She didn't physically act out and didn't break the rules. They didn't like her because she asked many questions. Many 'why' queries. Looking into it, I discovered there were no intentions of being rude; she merely did not accept what they said as the 'reality'. Thus, she would ask why things operated as they said."

"I listened in on several of the class discussions, and I did not perceive her dialogue as immediately placing judgment on them, but the professors sure did. The instructors considered her disrupting their lectures, disrespecting or rebelling against authority figures. Unfortunately, when one teacher says negative things about a student, word gets around the faculty fast. Because of this, she frequently faced disciplinary action like detention or referral to the principal's office," Mr. Dennison explained.

"Indeed. Victoria beamed with pride at having earned such a distinction," Ms. Walker added.

"I understand," Mansfield said, making a few notes in his notebook. "Did she ride the bus, walk, or drive to and from school?"

"Oh, she just got her driver's license this year. I assume she had to collect and transport her younger brother to all his extracurricular activities and games, so she dashed out the door. Part of the price paid for having a car," Ms. Walker answered.

"How involved with the schooling were Victoria's parents?" Mansfield asked.

Principal Dennison shook his head and said, "In the period Ms. Moody attended this school, I don't recall ever having met either. As absences occurred, we would leave messages as the law requires, but we never received a response."

"I tried to contact them many times this year out of concern for Victoria and the path she seemed to be pursuing. Despite my repeated attempts (by phone, mail, and other means), I have yet to receive a reply," Ms. Walker offered. "Her mother never tried to accommodate her father's frequent absences. High school is when parents often choose not to be involved in their children's education."

"In our investigation, we encountered a young man named Luca Medina. Do you know this individual?" Mansfield inquired. The principal and the counselor tensed, took deep breaths, and shared a look between them. Exhaling, they each relaxed in their respective chairs, independently shaking their heads.

"Luca is a sad story. He is one of mine I lost," Ms. Walker acknowledged. "What makes you ask about him? He was a student several years ago."

"His name came up in Victoria's computer and phone records. In one of her chats, he mentioned he went here for a while," the detective responded.

"Oh, well, this might explain a lot about her behavior this year if she had hooked up with him."

"Oh? Can you tell me a little about him?" Mansfield asked.

"Sure. Luca would be what… 21 or 22 by now? Back when he was still in school, he was everyone's crush. I'm sure you are familiar with these obsessive students from your school days. Anyway, all the girls adored him, but mostly from a distance. Anyone who got close to him usually found him odd and didn't stick around for long. He grew up with a father who drank excessively. Luca wasn't raised so much as he got older. He was one of our scholarship students."

Mansfield interrupted, "What do you mean they didn't stay around for long?"

"In some ways, Luca was a conundrum. He argued that people should be free to experience alternate realities. Luca strongly believed that nobody needed to conform to the standards set by the masses. Yet, in Luca's world, he lived by a strict code of ethics. He genuinely thought he was not subject to the norms and regulations of traditional society."

"This 'freedom of thought' appealed to many students, but when they pushed more into the notion, they discovered that it was terrifying," Ms. Walker tried to explain. A short pause and silence settled into the room. Mansfield attempted to reconcile his picture of Luca with the painted description.

"In what world did Luca think he belonged if not our world?"

"This is a question we could never answer. He never shared enough for us to understand," Principal Dennison said.

Ms. Walker sat with her chin down and her hands folded in her lap. Dennison exhibited shortness of breath. Mansfield detected a line of perspiration on his forehead and wondered if the man had just run a mental marathon.

"We attempted to contact his father, who never responded. We also tried to persuade him to seek counseling, but he rejected all our offers. I told him he needed to stop talking about such things on campus and reminded him that he was attending a Catholic school, but he still refused. As a result, six months before graduation, we had to expel him. I found the whole thing heartbreaking," Ms. Walker confessed while rubbing her hands together in her lap and trying to maintain eye contact with Mansfield.

"I understand he got his GED," Principal Dennison added.

Chapter 25

To her surprise, Sandra whirled around to see Mansfield standing there.

"Dave, you scared me to death." She leaned back against the occupied gurney to take a breath. "So you caught a rough one. Three DBs at one crime scene. Two of them were kids. That's tough. We finished the autopsies, vanilla, and you attended the formal IDs, so what brought you over to the morgue?" the medical examiner asked.

"Sandra, I need some help. We collected some vomit at the location, which we think is connected to the perp. There is at least a 60-day backlog on testing items obtained at crime scenes. By that time, this biological evidence may be unusable."

"Listen, Dave, the logjam includes gang shootings, floaters, sex offenders, etc. Does your case include anything that would make them prioritize you over everyone else in line?"

"For pity's sake, Sandra, mine is a triple homicide! Do I need anything more?"

"Go to your sergeant. Talk her into pushing the point."

"I tried. All she did was screw up her mouth, bite her lower lip, and bounce it back. You must have a couple of favors you can call in. I'm sitting at nothing tangible," Mansfield begged.

Sandra ranted, "The current DNA collection and analysis system needs improvement. These backlogs are because the labs are ill-equipped to handle the increasing influx of DNA samples and other items. They don't own the most up-to-date technology yet. More research is needed to develop faster methods for analyzing. Also, you folks in the field need more assistance to ensure the optimal use of DNA evidence to clear cases."

"Believe me, I understand. I attended a couple of these training sessions this year. President Bush believes we must do more to realize the full potential of DNA technology to solve crimes and has proposed millions in federal funding for this initiative. The financing is for five years and over a billion dollars. Nevertheless, this does not help me now, in this case," Dave pleaded again.

"All right, but only because of the kids, and you've got a triple. I can investigate what I can do. No promises." Sandra smiled at Mansfield and his intensity. She met him years ago, and her views of him have not changed since she first talked to him. She could spend hours gazing, catching glimpses of him. Sandra often encouraged him to leave the grind behind and pursue a career in filmmaking.

Mansfield showed up in the squad room sometime after five o'clock. He took the last sip of coffee from a Styrofoam cup and tossed the empty in the trash. Sergeant Johns left along with everyone else except Landers. He sat at his computer, finishing paperwork.

"Went by the high school today," Mansfield offered as he plopped down in his chair opposite Landers' desk. "Got an ear full about Luca Medina. The administration expelled the kid six months before graduation because he thought he was not subject to the same rules we are. Can you believe that one?"

"Yeppers. A background check says he got his GED and works as a DJ at the SOHO Lounge. He lives in Sunview Estates, South Miami. Clean sheet. A lot of the personal information I retrieved was from Victoria Moody's blog on her computer, where she writes about Luca a lot."

"She blogs about communities of self-identified vampires found around the world, including right here in Miami. Most of them keep to themselves and conduct their feeding rituals in private. Some of these proclaimed vampires do not ingest human blood but claim to feed off the energy of others."

"As she started referring to herself, Vicki said Luca belonged to a group called the House of Nuit Rouge. The heritage of this clan traces back to New Orleans. They consider themselves a coven. These 'vampires' are normal-seeming people who drink small amounts of blood to stay healthy."

Mansfield wrinkled his forehead and tilted his head slightly. "What in the hell is a blog?"

"Are you kidding? I'm talking about covens and shit like that, and the first thing you ask is—What is a blog?" Landers considered his companion and wondered how crap got processed in his head. With an exaggerated shake, he explained, "A blog is a diary, only written on a computer file. Her blog discusses being stuck between two forces who might want to harm her. There are the slayers on one side and Jade Holmes on the other."

"What the shit? What is a slayer?" Mansfield settled in for the lesson at hand.

"I looked it up. Never heard the term either. A slayer hunts down people who are or think they are vampires and kills them with a lot of emotion and violence. Similar to the *Buffy the Vampire Slayer* series."

"Are you shitting me?" Mansfield erupted in laughter. "Has the world gone insane? Who is Buffy? Would I like her?"

"Forget about Buffy, and no, you wouldn't like the program. Nonetheless, the presence of such individuals is a significant motivating factor for vampire-believing groups to conceal their existence. They are terrified of being slaughtered. Slayers are contract or serial killers who are just specific about who their victims are."

"Who is Jade Holmes? Is she a famous slayer or something?"

"No. Jade Holmes is a not-so-nice vampire. Vicki says she is an elder in the House of Alethia, a descendant of the larger covens in Buffalo. She considers it her job to anticipate slayers and thinks they hang around the other groups. Therefore, you are suspected if you do not belong to her faction and are not a vampire."

"Holmes runs a clandestine press that publishes unofficial information about the vampire citizenry. In these publications, she gives the names of those who need to be observed in case they are covert slayers," Landers summarized. "To keep her from publishing someone's name, another clan leader can declare a non-vampire person to be protected by the Dark Kiss. Everyone in the community is knowledgeable of who is safeguarded."

"Ridiculous! This sounds like a lose-lose scenario if what you describe occurs," Mansfield rattled. "If you are not named in the publication because the Dark Kiss covers you, then slayers are aware you are significant to a vampire because everyone in the surrounding communities knows about this, and you can become prey. Yet, assuming you are listed, the assassins know you are important to a community member, and you are still a target. Not a desirable outcome either way."

"Exactly. This is what Victoria is saying in her blog."

Chapter 26

"Now you've called, I am speechless. Bee never once entered my mind through all this," Peter groaned.

After he spoke with Jackie, Mansfield called Peter Ekker concerning Bee's visitors parked outside. The fact that Bee did not phone him didn't come as a surprise. Peter said things were heating up within the cartel, with daily trips to see Thomas becoming the norm. Everyone on his team remained vigilant to prevent the subsequent murder. Chatter indicated the hit would be on American soil this time.

"Well, at Thomas' warehouse a few years back, she did witness two of the guys' exchange sacks full of cash. In my ideal world, they would have forgotten about the elderly lady Thomas said suffered from Alzheimer's," Mansfield grumbled. "Nevertheless, one can never tell."

"I am all too aware of the situation, which is unfortunate. I just sent a car to her place right away," Peter said.

"For the past two nights, I noted a car positioned in front of her place, watching and recording activity around Freedom Pointe. The occupants didn't act friendly. Last night I called the precinct and asked them to do a drive-by. The car packed up and left," Mansfield bragged. "Do you still have eyes on Thomas?"

"You bet we do. His every move is recorded. As I said, it's a matter of time before this gets settled."

Dave made a point of stopping at Jackie's house instead of just driving by. An uneasy notion in his stomach made itself known, and he wanted to check things for himself. Being an only child often means taking on extra responsibilities. With his knock on the door, Jackie answered, and a moment of déjà vu punched him and took his breath away. His mother stood in the doorway, all dressed up, holding a glass of wine, and the other attendees at the dinner party laughed in the other room. Perhaps in a parallel dimension, he thought he had been here before.

He started to recite the Serenity Prayer in his head but did not finish. She pounced on him like a predator, delighted to see him, snatched him by the arm, and all but dragged him into the dining room. Her guests included Bee, Caspar, and Gregory, a friend his mother met at her tai chi class. After the introductions, Bee and Jackie went in to prepare dessert. The friend and Caspar began conversing while Mansfield sat back to survey and assess.

"The new restaurant we tried the other night proved to be amazing. I can give my highest praise," Caspar commented.

"What is the place called?"

Caspar thought for a minute and said, "What is the name of the president's wife who got assassinated? The one in Dallas?" Considering how unexpected this question sounded, Mansfield's curiosity detector went off. He shifted in his seat and listened.

"Do you mean John F. Kennedy? He married Jackie. Why?" Gregory inquired, puzzled.

"Yes, that's the one," He turned toward the kitchen and yelled, "Jackie, what's the name of the cafe we went to?"

Dave sat back and made mental notes. Caspar, or whatever his name is, should attend a short-term memory loss group. Otherwise, he had heard this joke a hundred times before.

"So who drove to the diner?" Mansfield asked.

"Oh, we took her car. I am so old that my driving terrifies people." The girls entered the room in time to hear this, and everyone laughed.

Jackie's son joined in but wasn't feeling the vibe. His instincts told him that Caspar was exerting too much effort. He appeared to be enacting elderly stereotypes he probably laughed at as a young man. Many warning signs emerged while seated next to Gregory. Mansfield wanted to kick himself.

For the first time, Dave saw his mother's boyfriend through the eyes of a detective and discovered things he didn't like. On closer inspection, he did not appear as old as he wanted people to think, and now he had a point of reference to be compared with. Caspar's hands were younger and less veiny, he displayed neck strength, and his eyes, well, the energy in his eyes was too bright. He retained an upright body position and moved with intent.

Gregory, who had thin skin and a forward-bending stance, walked slowly, communicated carefully, and maintained a reflective perception. The most prominent example of Caspar's incongruous behavior centered around his excessive attention to Jackie, but he failed to remember her name. How does that work?

Through coffee and cake, Bee confessed to acquiring a puppy. At the beginning of the quarter, the Pointe had changed its rules, and if you lived in the apartments, you could own a pet that weighed up to 25 pounds. This weight climbed to 50 for those staying in a cabin. The three-month-old yellow Labrador Retriever named Sadie became Bee's new companion.

"Sadie has so much spirit and such an outgoing personality. She is warm and affectionate but chews on everything. This pup goes through bones as fast as I go through toilet paper. Bee was happy and excited about her new roommate. The first thing on my list of things to do is to get her some training. Everything is perfect."

No one bothered to tell her the dog wouldn't be under 50 pounds for long. After this news, the men left for the evening, and Dave stayed to talk with the ladies.

"So, Bee, I understand you didn't call Mr. Ekker at the Drug Enforcement Agency. Why didn't you advise him that someone had been watching your home?" Dave asked.

"I don't trust them. Anyone who makes a living doing all that crap every day is bound to have bad stuff in their past."

"And what, you think whatever those skeletons are might be worse than having hitmen sitting in your driveway?" Mansfield said, dripping with sarcasm.

Jackie had to jump in, "Now, Dave, there is no evidence to suggest they are professional killers. Why would you say something like that? You are scaring her. Stop."

"Mom, she needs to be scared. Why do you believe they're here if they're not assassins? They work with Thomas daily, so they are mindful of his whereabouts. He's been doing business with them for over three years. Why are they showing up now?"

Everyone stood in the kitchen. No one wanted to be the first to talk. Bee turned and finished putting dishes in the dishwasher while Jackie and her son just stared at her.

"Listen, Bee. Peter spent 10 years on the Miami police force before I ever moved here. For the next five years, we worked near one another. He left to infiltrate Mexico's violent cartels with the DEA. I've been his associate for a long time."

"He talks about pretending to be a trafficker, setting up cocaine deals, and working to take down corrupt soldiers. His favorite story is about one of his missions in Mexico, where he and one of his informants visited two dealers at a fast-food establishment. He was purchasing marijuana. Almost two hours had passed, and the Mexican federal officers surrounding the joint were getting nervous."

"As darkness descended, one of the traffickers went outdoors, and Peter followed. A Mexican official stepped out of the shadows and put a gun to the trafficker's chest, and things began to go wrong. The trafficker grabbed the firearm and shot the officer in the head."

"Peter would detail how dark red blood darted up, and then the dealer turned the weapon on him. Peter was about three feet away when the villain fired two rounds. Peter could hear the bullets whistle in his ear. He says all this happened in seconds, and he killed the miscreant. All hell hit the pavement. I am telling you this because I want you to understand that he is an officer of the law and has often been in demanding situations. He is a man of decisive action."

"Now, Peter is a licensed DEA pilot. He works from the Intelligence Center in Miami, which oversees policing and monitoring duties near the Gulf border." Mansfield watched his mother and Bee, hoping they would understand Ekker was on their side.

Chapter 27

She went to the hotel's seventh floor and headed to the door she had walked to so many Friday afternoons before. As the day faded, the sunlight streaming through the window told its story. Lee ambled lazily about the room, tracing her index finger across the dresser below the mirror. She paused before the decorative framed-looking glass and studied her reflection, which included the king bed and nightstands.

With perfect precision, the duvet cover, down comforter, six pillows, and three Euro shams all stood at attention, just as they had every time before. Everything looked familiar except for the face staring back at her. Her unfocused gaze pondered the details of her own life, which left an indelible impression despite its relative brevity.

Lee turned toward the bed and leaned on the dresser. She told Evie, "You strolled into the room like a god, and I thought about how I'd stumbled across you that evening so long ago. In all honesty, I assumed you'd approach others. But fate triumphed over probability because you walked right up to me. You gave me so much self-confidence that I went out and actively pursued an academic profession."

She pulled the curtains, blocking the sunlight and the outside world despite the room's breathtaking vista. Premium wines, spirits, mixers, and artisans' delicacies embellished the hotel's minibar. They never ate the refreshments. Lee prepared a drink and relaxed in the lounge chair, allowing the liquor to work magic. She stared at the bed. Which emotion did she feel most: anger or grief? After her third cocktail, the lost lover started talking to Evie again.

"If only you understood the struggles that I overcame to meet you. You don't understand who I am or what I went through. I'm now curious if you ever cared. Back when I answered to the name Beverly, oh, you were never aware of those days. I once told my mom that I liked girls more than boys. She was the only person I ever told before I met you. She told me sentiments like these are common, but I should keep them to myself to avoid rejection."

"I listened to her for 20 years, and here you go and prove her right. Not long after I told her, she killed herself. Yep. That's right. Simply put, my dad was a good ole boy, causing her to swallow an entire bottle of pills. After the funeral, he informed me that because my mother committed suicide over my decision to attend college, I needed to spend the rest of my life picking up where she left off. It wasn't true, but you would have been proud of me. I fixed his ass."

Lee sat and fought back the tears that spilled down her face. Her anger had brought her this far, but now she was about to give up. Her life had become impossible. She refilled her drink and turned, surveying her surroundings again. The room had turned gloomy, chilly, and nearly black. Time passed regardless of what she was going through inside. The place was silent and solemn. An involuntary shiver attacked her body, and she felt raw as the shadows surrounded her.

It was distinct, penetrating darkness caused by the lack of light, almost beckoning. Following her original instincts, she took a few steps to flee toward the curtains and snatch them open. However, she stopped midway, realizing the dark outside would not provide solace. Instead, she climbed on the bed, clutched a pillow, and brought her knees to her chin.

The warmth of the coverlet resting over the bottom of the bed temporarily relieved her uneasiness. Lee's heart ached with an unknown pain, and she reached mindlessly across the bed to touch Evie, but no one was there. Not anymore. She sensed warm water droplets on her skin and realized her eyes had betrayed her. She also detected something pulling her deeper into the darkness. This was different from how things should have played out.

Her heart broke, and she let out a sob she'd suppressed for too long. She felt drawn into the abyss until her emotions were swept up as part of a category-five hurricane. Her ticker raced, her lungs closed, and she became petrified of what might happen. The room warmed, and the tossing and twisting in her thoughts ceased just as she began to think all hope might be lost.

The darkness remained, but she didn't want to open her eyes. Lee scanned her body mentally and found she seemed okay. However, an emotional void remained as her body calmed. Instead of experiencing her emotions, she opted for numbness.

As a jilted lover, she realized she was completely submerged in her sorrow. Now that things were more straightforward, she could see she had been misled. She reflected on the precise moment she had her epiphany. Evie had been complaining about how much money and freedom her husband had taken from her. She wanted to escape her humdrum existence and see the world as a reward for all her demanding work.

I thought you were letting off some steam when you told me how frustrating your daughter sometimes got. I didn't believe you meant everything you said. The thought that you would consider leaving Cooper never entered my mind. Later, you start giving me leaflets about migrating to a European province or territory and telling me we must produce a plan because Europe is great. You started drafting divorce papers, and I found out. I became so pumped because I thought you might be legit. I packed my bags and was ready to leave the United States to start a new life.

She looked over to where Evie would lay, "Next, without notice, you informed me we weren't a good match. To put things another way: I was too perfect for you, so you didn't want to take me to Europe with you. You thought I was too dense to see through your deception and evasiveness. Even at my advanced age of 40-plus, I desperately wished I could vanish."

Lee looked up at the ceiling, focused on the fire sprinkler, and wondered why she wanted her back so much.

Chapter 28

He showered, shaved, and wore any of the dark, similar suits in his closet. After clipping his Glock to his belt, the detective headed to the diner for coffee, fried eggs, and grits. He took Collins Avenue north, then left on 11th Street, and his mouth salivated as he read the 'Breakfast-All-Day' sign. At 7:30 on a Saturday morning, he represented one of the few people awake and hungry.

Satisfied after feasting and flirting with the waitstaff, Mansfield only needed a cigarette to top everything off. He removed the package from his pocket, studied it, and finally replaced it. His tooth's condition had significantly improved, and maintaining this was critical. He took his coffee and drove the quickest route to the downtown MPD. Vehicle traffic was picking up.

On the way to his desk, he nodded at a few fellow officers and proceeded to the shelf behind Landers' workspace to grab the Moody Murder Book. Mansfield preferred the quiet of a Saturday morning in the clubhouse. Yes, people mulled around, but the overall energy level remained focused. Often, the brass was nowhere to be seen.

Every morning he tried to catch up on the latest updates, but if he had free time on a weekend morning, he would start at the beginning. With this method, he uncovered previously overlooked finer details. His ability to draw conclusions and formulate hypotheses helped guide his actions. Revitalized, he could zero in on the case as additional clues and information became available.

Landers had the day off but had left his notes regarding the background check of Charles Gray. Mansfield peered at the picture, seeing a black-skinned man with trimmed, wavy, inky black hair, and mahogany brown eyes, and he appeared to be of average weight and a little thin and a little short, but not noticeably so. Nothing about this man's appearance stood out as unusual or peculiar. The photo portrayed someone ordinary and forgettable.

Mr. Gray had a legitimate social security number. His listed occupation was as a chef, and he worked at the City of Miami Fire Station No. 1. Mansfield leaned back in his chair to reflect on this odd piece of information. *How does one end up being a hash slinger for a bunch of firefighters and emergency technicians? Does he have the same training as they do, or is he just a cook?* While taking notes, he became aware of someone approaching from behind. He turned.

"Oh, hi, Rita. Thanks for coming in. Landers took the day off, but there are some outstanding issues in the Moody case that I want to jump on. I appreciate you hanging out with me. How did the detective exam go?" Mansfield inquired.

"Not as horrible as I anticipated, but I have earned a criminal justice degree and worked as a patrol officer for a decade. With all this, I still studied."

"Once you pass, what department are you going for?" Interested, he put down the papers in his hand.

"Homicide detective is my ultimate career objective although I understand it may be necessary to gain skills in other fields first."

"Good for you. You're in the right place for some practical experience. I'm reviewing the murder book and looking at the summaries Landers left regarding Charles Gray. Jump in. We can leave as soon as I'm done with these notes."

Landers' notes indicated that the suspect earned his GED at the age of 20 and worked in the food service industry to make money as a young man. He took cooking lessons at night school. Things must have gone well because job hopping and minimum wage earnings stopped when he took a position as an apprentice chef at Jan Jensen's, an establishment that debuted in South Miami in 1992. In 1999, Charles left the restaurant and went to work as a cook for the fire station.

Mansfield fixed two coffees to go and put the files he wanted to take together. Slater followed right behind him. In less than 10 minutes, they twisted and turned their way to the firehouse. With no active fires or incoming calls, firefighters were available for additional duties at the fire station. The most significant appeared to be taking inventory and doing equipment checks. The officers walked into the area and approached the first person they encountered: a fireman hunched over a tool compartment on one of the vehicles. His broad, muscular back displayed the muscles straining against the fabric of his shirt.

"Hello. We are with the Miami Police Department and are here to talk with Mr. Charles Gray." The firefighter whom they interrupted stood and turned around. To Mansfield's surprise, the sizable guy welcomed them with a broad grin rather than the hostility he had anticipated.

"You would be amazed at how much gear gets carried on this truck. I mean that it must be checked regularly to guarantee everything is there, in excellent condition, and operational. It can be boring, but necessary to make sure the right tools are in working order when we need them." The firefighter wiped his hands and offered to shake. "I'm sorry I didn't catch your names, but Charles isn't here today. Saturday is his day off."

"I'm Detective Mansfield, and this is Officer Slater," they shook the man's big hand.

"Oh. I'm Lars Ahmad. Is there anything I can do for you?"

"No. We need to speak with Mr. Gray. How long have you worked with him?"

"I guess about five years since we hired him."

"What are his duties around here?"

"Well, he does all the cooking. He is a fabulous cook, and we dine like kings. For the mealtimes when he is not here, he prepares meals for us to reheat. We seldom eat leftovers, and the food is always fresh. We all groan when he's not around."

"Does he do anything else? Does he go out on calls, or does he help with the equipment or anything like that?" Mansfield continued his questions.

"No. He spends his time meal planning, shopping, and cooking. He is addicted to caffeine because he's always carrying a coffee or a Pepsi."

"Does he talk much about his life outside the station or his past?" Slater interjected.

"Not much. He usually keeps to himself. You can catch him rambling if you hang out in the kitchen long enough, but only if he's had more than a few drinks. One afternoon, I tried to speak to him about his childhood and where he came from, just trying to bond. The most he said was that he came from a dying village close to a forest and had risked his life to escape. He said he would never go back. He can be dramatic."

"Does he ever spend the night here?"

"Oh, yes. He has a bunk, and I think he gets lonely when his roommate goes out of town. After the evening meal, he sleeps over when this occurs. I love it when he stays because he will usually whip up something wonderful for a bedtime snack." Lars answered while licking his lips and thinking about the food.

"Can we glimpse his working space and his room?" The detective requested in a tone that did not sound like a question.

"Of course." The firefighter led Mansfield and Slater to the kitchen area of the firehouse and pointed in the direction of Charles' sleeping accommodations.

"Do you remember if Charles slept over last Tuesday evening?"

"Tuesday night, yeah, I'm sure we were both here. I don't recall anything unusual, but I can conjure up the fabulous breakfast prepared on Wednesday morning. He made every effort to impress!"

By necessity, the kitchen was small, with aged appliances, press-board cabinets, and uneven floors. "A galley, perhaps eight by 10 feet. Simple. Charles has utilized the available area to achieve maximum productivity," Mansfield noted.

Slater nodded in agreement. "I love horizontal pulls. They double as dishtowel hanging space." She went over and addressed one of the bottomless compartments. "I can't believe it's full of pots and pans. Think about that, using deep drawers to keep cookware unseen." She opened one of the smaller bins. "Over here, this one is outfitted with cutlery dividers, allowing the counter to stay clutter-free. I love it."

Mansfield observed the whole of the galley. "The limited floor space requires the cabinets in this kitchen to extend to the lofty height of eight feet. I wonder how Charles gets to these hard-to-reach storage areas. A stepladder must be somewhere." He gazed around and couldn't find where the steps would be stored nearby.

While checking the cabinets, Slater found a bottom door next to the refrigerator. She leaned over but was unable to pull open the drawer. "Dave, this door is odd. Do you think it is a fake?"

Mansfield walked over and stared down at the board. "Move over a sec." He kicked the panel square in the center and out popped a folding stepladder.

"Damn," Slater mumbled. "Humph. Well, this is a substantial fridge. It is significant enough for batch cooking. I would cook in this kitchen."

"Let's examine the sleeping accommodations," Mansfield said as he walked off.

The bunk room was conveniently located next to the galley, which was like a walk-in pantry, tiny and tidy. Nothing but a twin bed, a night table with a lamp and alarm clock, and a small closet about half the size of those found in Motel 8. At first, the wardrobe appeared empty, but Mansfield unearthed a surprise upon inspecting the dark corners.

"Well, well, well. Look see here?"

Slater turned from the nightstand to find out what he meant. Her heart skipped a beat. "No, did that come from the walk-in?"

"Yeppers." He stood still, facing his partner of the day, holding a Winchester pump 12-gauge. The detective walked further into the light. "You know what, this is a collector's piece. Model 12 is short for Model 1912, the year they went into production. They stopped making these in the mid-sixties. Curious to find a shotgun like this here, among Gray's stuff."

Mansfield took the weapon straight to the car and locked it in the trunk. Slater found a few more firefighters and verified that they remembered Charles sleeping over Tuesday night. No one recalled what he did all evening, but they all confirmed he had dinner, slept in his bunk, and made a magnificent breakfast Wednesday morning. For most, the morning meal stirred the recall.

Chapter 29

Mansfield and Slater jumped on the MacArthur Causeway and headed for Miami Beach, where Charles Gray and Mark Moody lived. According to protocol, the shotgun was in the trunk until it could be submitted as evidence. Dave and Rita went straight to the open elevator. She looked at the bank of numbers while he took up residence in the elevator's center, the formidable detective waiting for a confrontation. The doors closed, and she looked over at him, disheartened.

"The number is not listed. Look, some of the floors are missing."

Mansfield looked at her and sighed, inhaling and exhaling slowly. Slater recognized one of Mansfield's signature moves, the six-second pause. Why six seconds? She reasoned it was because the chemistry of emotions in the human brain and body only survives for about six seconds.

If he could wait for a moment, the flood of chemicals being produced would slow down. Therefore, when he is frustrated or upset before he says something harsh, this hesitation helps him assess the costs and benefits of his action. This allows him to make careful choices. She did not want to rush him.

Mansfield reached over, pushed the open-door button, and exited the elevator. He announced his arrival to the gatekeeper, who walked them to a 'special elevator'. The door attendant used a 'special' key and a 'secret' code, telling the lift to take them to the floor where Moody and Gray lived. All this pretense did nothing but irritate the detective further.

On the ride up, Mansfield muttered, "Within 10 seconds, they will reveal all they claim to know. What a waste of time." Other apartments on the VIP level hindered their way, and by the time they located the correct one, the door stood open.

"Hello, Detective. I find it great to reconnect with you. Please come in," Mark cooed.

"Good afternoon, Mr. Moody. This is Officer Slater, in case you don't recall." Mark and Rita shook hands, and everyone entered the condominium. "We are here to speak with Charles Gray. Does he happen to be home?"

"Why yes, of course. Why do you need to talk with him?"

"Can you advise him we are here?"

"Charles, the MPD is here for you?" He ambled out of the back room. His arrogance almost superseded Mark's.

"Are you Charles Gray, who resides at this address?" The detective demanded.

"Why yes, of course. What can I do for you?" Charles crowed. Mansfield desperately wanted to tackle these guys.

"In light of recent developments, we have a few questions for you regarding events that took place on the evening of Tuesday, October 19th. We should take this inquiry downtown to the station."

Mark interrupted, "Oh no, ask them here. I am working in the other room."

"Yes, here is fine," Charles added.

"This is a beautiful day. Let's talk out on the balcony for a little privacy," Slater stated as she moved toward the sliding glass doors and the sundeck. Gray and Mansfield followed her. The door was closed before Mark had a chance to follow.

"So may I call you Charles?" Mansfield started. He shook his head in affirmation. "How did you meet Mark Moody?"

"I worked as a waiter in a restaurant, trying to earn enough for rent and cooking courses to become a culinarian and make more money. He liked me and was a generous tipper. He came back often. When he found out I was working to pay my way through school, he started helping with the tuition. When I completed most of my classes, he got me a job at Jan Jensen's as an apprentice chef. His help blew my mind. We became close, and I moved in with him in 1999."

"What about his wife and family? Did he tell you about them?"

"Sure, but he didn't like them. He would rather be with me or traveling and doing his music thing. She always threatened him with stuff with no intention of following through. She just enjoyed making him miserable. I reassured him that he had no reason to worry about her, as the two of us had now connected and could face any challenge as a team. Her most recent event, the bitch, was a divorce. She sent him the papers before he went on tour in Austria."

"So Mark found out about the breakup?" Slater interjected. Mansfield faked boredom with the subject.

"Naturally, I told him. I feared he might damage himself. He grabbed the keys and tried to drive to the house, but I wouldn't let him. So he stayed but kept ranting and pacing. His external aggression then took over. The shouting and swearing ended up with a hole in the wall in our bedroom. Things are still a mess." Charles shook his head back and forth. "I tell you, Evie had me so furious."

"A breakup sounds like a nice solution if he didn't like them, and neither did you. Why did you react this way?" Slater said, puzzled and confused.

"Are you kidding? In this case, money was the driving factor. Mark would lose a lot in the divorce. She wanted child support for the older child, wanted to dump the younger kid on him, and wanted all the accumulated wealth. She claimed none of her assets or income from Trendsetter should be involved since the agency belonged to her before marriage. Now the business throws off millions of dollars. She makes much more money than he does. Her net worth well surpasses his. He didn't understand why she couldn't leave things be."

"Charles, where are you from? You have an accent I'm not familiar with." Mansfield said, changing the subject.

"Oh, I'm from the swamps in western upstate New York. I stayed until I could escape, left, and came to Miami."

"My family has mentioned some kin in that part of the state. What borough did you grow up in?" Dave baited.

"My mom was originally from the Shinnecock, and I journeyed to the west coast of NY when I was little with her. I'm not familiar with the county. Guess I never cared."

Slater flipped through her notebook under the pretense of looking something up and followed with a note in her notepad. She looked up and asked, "Charles, does this mean you have only been to New York and Miami? You have never been anyplace else in the United States?"

"Correct. Never wanted to go anywhere else. Not much of a traveler. Traveling is for Mark, not me." Mansfield glanced at her with curiosity and avoided her question.

The melody inside burst forth like a pent-up flood. Like moonlight, Dave envisioned Moody's hands brushing the keys with velvet grace. The sound was breathtaking. Mark was worried about his companion. His feeble attempt at distraction drew more attention to Charles and reinforced the importance of the relationship between the two.

"On Tuesday, October 19, how did you spend the afternoon and night?" Slater quizzed, changing subjects again.

"Mark's work took him to Austria. I don't much care for an empty house. So I spent the night at the fire station."

"Can anyone verify your claims?"

"I think on-duty people should be able to. The evening was quiet. No calls."

"Is Charles Gray your real name?" the detective asked, looking up from his notebook and meeting the man eye-to-eye.

"Honestly, no. Since I didn't want to continue using the name I was called in the swamps, I assumed this one after I made it out."

"Please tell me your 'swamp name'?" Mansfield encouraged; hopeful progress was being made.

"Suflet Intunecat."

"What does it mean?" Slater jumped in.

"No idea."

"Are you a US citizen?" Mansfield followed up.

"I think so. Yes."

"Do you own a gun of any make or model?" Again, Mansfield stared his suspect down.

After a pause, no more than one or two seconds, Charles replied, "No."

Chapter 30

Mansfield left The Yacht Club and took Collins Avenue to 11th Street. He pulled into the diner and looked over at Rita.

"One of the best places on the island," the detective smiled. He unlocked the trunk and took out a blank MPD report form to show Slater this was a working lunch. His and Rita's notebooks would provide good details and information to transcribe the interview with Charles Gray to the form using police parlance.

"What did you trigger on when he said he had only been in New York and Miami?" Mansfield asked.

"Remember this morning, at the station house, when you wanted to finish reviewing the notes before we left? My eyes swept over Charles's SSN as I reviewed his biographical details. I was playing around, to tell the truth. However, I studied the components of how the Social Security Administration assigns numbers in preparation for the exam. So I tried to read his."

"What do you mean the parts and pieces?"

"The first three digits of a person's identification number indicate the region in which the person originally applied for the number. These numbers constitute a unique identifier for every area inside a state, as each district is assigned a code and ID. The East Coast uses lower integers, whereas the West uses greater ones. I'm sure you don't care much about the rest of the training."

"Damn. Look at you."

"Yeah, so when I looked up his at the station, the digits on his SSN came up somewhere in northern California. Therefore, when he said he had never been anywhere except New York and Miami, all sorts of bells went off. Either he lied, or his social security number is false." Slater looked at Mansfield and smiled.

"Nice. We need to ask Landers to check this right away. He also didn't tell the truth about living with the Shinnecock. I'm sure they had finished migrating by his birth."

"Where do you think he came up with a 'swamp name' like—Suflet Intunecat?" Slater referred to her notes, "Isn't it kind of weird he would have something like this right off the top of his head?"

"Yes, which means what he said is likely true. However, the name denotes something in another dialect. His accent is Eastern European. I'm not sure; maybe Slovak. At the very least, he has trouble pronouncing some sounds, like the letter 'T'. English is not his first language. We should also investigate this."

"To finish up the report, we have the lie of all lies, the shotgun in the trunk he says he does not own," Slater snickered.

"Yes, but first, we must verify that this gun is the one we're after. Then, we can trace the weapon back to him if necessary. He can say the piece isn't his and, therefore, must belong to any of the firefighters roaming around the fire station," her colleague cautioned.

After dropping Slater, the gun, and the Gray report off at the squad room, Mansfield made for Luca Medina's place. Sundown Estates was about an hour's trip, so he jumped on the Dolphin Expressway and headed west. He used this drive time to review what he read about Luca from the background check, Victoria's computer, and the interview at the high school.

After entering the subdivision, Dave slowed down and cautiously looked around. Despite the mature trees and bushes, the poor condition of the neighborhood's roads and walkways indicated their age. The area appeared typical of South Miami's low-income, working-class neighborhoods, dreary and disheartening.

On the positive side, street corners were absent of kids standing around with nothing to do. He drove up to Luca's address, a sad little tubular duplex with a yard comprised mostly of sand and sprigs of grass clinging to life. Unlike many other dwellings, no one sat outside taking in the breeze, and the front door remained shut. Closed windows and curtains pulled tight warned intruders to stay away.

Mansfield knocked. Seconds passed until the door cracked open. Cool air assaulted him, trying to escape into this cruel world. Music played low, and a pair of penetrating green eyes from the chiseled face of a young man stared out to survey who dared interrupt his solitude.

The detective announced himself and his purpose and held his badge to the six-inch opening. The eyes shifted, the door closed, and chains rattled. Once opened, Mansfield entered and stepped to the side. From behind, he jumped slightly at the creaking and slamming of the door.

"Mr. Medina, thank you so much for agreeing to speak with me." Luca smiled and shook the detective's hand. He welcomed his visitor inside and invited him to sit on the old couch. The odor of wet socks brought back memories of Dave's time at the police academy when he had to spend weeks training for the physical fitness exam.

Mansfield looked around as he followed Luca and noted that one wall held a poster of someone called Siouxsie and the Banshees. The only notable features of the space included a few pieces of flea market furniture and some high-end stereo equipment. He rethought Medina and settled on mold or mildew instead of the typical manly workout scent.

"Would you like something to drink?" Luca offered.

"Oh, no, thank you," he replied. Instead of parking his rump on the couch, he toppled into it. Sitting next to the arm helped him maintain a more upright stance. Luca pulled a chair in from the kitchen and sat opposite the officer.

"Luca, may I call you by your first name?" Mansfield asked. He nodded his permission.

"So you are quite a connoisseur of technology and music?"

"Oh yes. What can I say? That's my profession. Since I'm a disc jockey, sound is my livelihood."

"I understand now. Is this one of your preferred artists? I don't believe I have ever run across him?" Mansfield asked, indicating the poster on the wall.

"Her. Siouxsie is female. Yes, she is. It is Dark Wave, a genre that emerged in the 1970s and is my favorite. Most of it is called New Wave or Post Punk. What type of tunes do you like to listen to?"

"Who me, I'm an old fella. Country all the way. This New or Punk or whatever: does it have songs about vampires and the like?" Mansfield asked, looking directly at Luca.

Surprised by the detective's directness, Luca's body tensed. "Well, yes, some. But a great deal of the stuff is not cultish."

"Oh. How did you meet Victoria Moody?"

"Over the Internet," Luca answered. He continued to give the investigator the complete story, which matched Victoria's blog. The detective sat and listened, giving him his time to talk.

"Were you guys a couple, or was the relationship casual?" Mansfield asked.

"Nothing formal, but we considered ourselves an item. I did not date anyone else, and I'm sure Vicki didn't either," Luca answered. His eyes started to water.

"Did you have the opportunity to meet her parents?"

"No. She never wanted me to. She avoided them at all costs since she did not like them. Vicki told me they were divorcing, but it didn't matter because her father never stayed at the same place as her mom. Her only interest centered on her little brother. She wanted to shield him by keeping him away from the house. We would attend his games, feed him, and otherwise look after him. She did her best to be like a second mother because the real mother never tended to these functions."

"What did you think of her mom and dad?"

"After the children hit puberty, Vicki said they started pushing them away. They continued treating them like kids, never allowing them to grow and gain respect. She hated her mother since she gave her the silent treatment if she didn't call in regularly. She had to leave a message most of the time. As a younger child, she understood this, but as she got older, she wanted more independence."

"Also, the criticism became a problem. Evie would pick holes in her character, while Mark, when around, would attempt to defend her. Vicki gave up and found excuses to avoid returning to the house. Although she was a good student through the tenth grade, her mother never encouraged her to continue. Grades were a non-event in the household."

"Nonetheless, the crucial factor was the unsettling nature of the household because everyone always seemed stressed about something. Her parents argued until the dad left when Evie retreated to her bedroom. The kids absorbed their parents' negative energy throughout their daily lives. Of course, this is my opinion, knowing all my information came from one tainted source. I didn't come from the best home environment, and I related to some stuff she would tell me."

"Can you think of anyone who would want to hurt Victoria?" Mansfield uttered.

"No, not really. The people she hung out with at school appeared harmless. Other than them, the only people she had anything to do with were me and Cooper. And we loved her," Luca sniffed.

"Was Victoria aware of your vampirism?" the detective circled back around with a more direct question this time.

"No, not at first. I kept the condition from her for a long time, but…" Luca paused, dropped his head, and started fiddling with his fingers in his lap. Dave sat silently through the pause.

"I told her about the community, the coven, and vampire life. I became so afraid I would lose her if I didn't tell her, but I realized I most likely would if I did. I gambled and told her everything."

"And her response?"

Luca got up and walked into the kitchen to blow his nose. He came back with a clean tissue and sat down. "She declared her love for me and her desire to be a part of us. How shocking is that! She thought vampire clubs existed for you to join. I had to explain to her that vampirism was something you had since birth, not something you decided to do," Luca laughed to himself and blew his nose again.

"Luca, can you think of anyone from your group who might want to hurt Victoria?" the investigator pushed with ease.

Luca looked up, his eyes glistening from heartbreak. "Two: the leader of the other community or a slayer," Luca explained who and where Jade Holmes could be located and articulated a slayer's purpose in life. Mansfield made many notes in his official notebook.

"Good. This is good, Luca. Do you have an alibi for Tuesday, 10/19?"

"I worked the entire night. The SOHO Lounge. You should be able to verify with management. I guess you guys always check out the boyfriend, don't you?"

"Yes. One last question. Do you own a gun?"

"Absolutely not."

"Luca, I must ask. Everyone is a suspect until they aren't." Luca nodded, indicating he understood, and walked the detective to the door.

Chapter 31

The first chilly spell of the season appeared, announcing that autumn had arrived. Overnight lows hit the high-fifties, and the highs reached the low-mid-seventies. The sporadic afternoon thundershowers characteristic of Florida's climate contributed to below-average rainfall. Yet, on this splendid Sunday, everything was fresh and invigorating, a delight to the senses. No clouds were in sight, and the sky was a more vibrant blue than the previous week.

On days like today, Freedom Pointe residents rode their golf carts down the trail to the square, marketed as a convenience. Since rent included most necessities, the shopping center was for enjoyment only. A drugstore, Hallmark Cards, a Dollar General, and two other tiny shops anchored the area if pensioners wanted to shop.

Jackie felt a growing restlessness, leading to a survey of her cottage and the decision that today would be a good day to take a cart ride to the marketplace. She called Maggie and asked whether she was up for going on the trip with her since she knew Bee wouldn't leave Sadie for so long. Living in the tower apartments, Jackie drove over to pick her up and down the path they went.

The avenue remained covered with a thin canopy that hinted at a once green but now brownish covering. She raised her eyes to the tree cover above and was glad to view a cloudless sky. She hoped scattered leaves would be on the sidewalk tomorrow. No doubt, this was her preferred time of year.

Maggie was an avid reader. She had already devoured all the books at Freedom Pointe since she made most of the contributions to the Freedom Pointe library. As Jackie enjoyed the outdoors, her Canasta partner chattered about her latest novel. Stephen King was one of her favorite authors, and she followed the Gunslinger series beginning in 1982.

The seventh and final publication, *The Dark Tower*, now had her undivided attention. This is the book where the author draws the epic tale about the last gunslinger in the world to a close, pulling all the pieces of the puzzle together. Obsessed with this chronology and often known to debate the upcoming conclusion, Maggie was in her world. As the driver, Jackie tuned her out.

Jackie picked up some dog toys for Sadie at Dollar General without thought. The thought of why she did things like this plagued her. She did not care for dogs and loathed cats; thus, she disapproved of Bee getting a puppy. Even so, she bought them and decided it would be a nice gesture. The movie theater played one motion picture at a time, and today it was the comedy *Taxi*, starring Queen Latifah. The girls opted to take in the hour-and-a-half-long feature.

Still laughing, the girls walked out of the movie. "I thought I would die when Belle told Andy, 'We've gotta play to your strengths. And thinkin' ain't one of them.' That Queen Latifah cracks me up."

Jackie sensed a change as the air cooled. A chilly breeze buffeted her face, and she shuddered without control. She pulled her scarf closer and fastened her sweater. The shadows became longer as the sun sank below the horizon. After dropping Maggie off at the main door, she took off for home, but as she turned up her street, she spotted police and ambulance lights above her cabin.

She drove up in her cart to check out the commotion and discovered vehicles around Bee's place. Her stomach churned as she thought of Dave's warnings. She heard Sadie's crazy barking. She arrived as the hospital wagon departed and frantically questioned many officers about the incident. Nothing, including the name of the place where the paramedics were going.

Soon, she gave up and dialed her son. Of course, she needed to leave messages. She made sure they were emergency communications. Having received her message from three diverse sources, Mansfield immediately returned Jackie's call.

"Dave, I don't understand what's going on. I just returned from the marketplace, and the ambulance is taking Bee away. No one answers me. The dog is in the house going berserk, and I'm confused about what they are doing. I am so worried. What should I do?"

"Are you hurt in any way, Mom?" Mansfield probed.

"No. I'm fine. I was with Maggie and got back in time to see the taillights of the ambulance going down the road. The officers are still here, making me stand behind some yellow tape."

"Good. Calm down. Go home, so you don't make yourself sick. I am on my way," Dave promised. Mansfield called the City of Coral Gables Police Department, identified himself, and asked about the event in progress at Freedom Pointe. He indicated that his mother lived in a couple of cabins from the call, and he was on his way to the scene. He would arrive in about 40 minutes.

The Grease dicks caught the case. Dave rolled his eyes. They were not his favorites, but at least they would do the job. Since Sandy and Danny were their given names, the Grease detectives got their nicknames from the characters from the 1978 film *Grease*, starring John Travolta and Olivia Newton-John. Mansfield put in a call to Danny D to get the lowdown on the crime scene.

"This afternoon, an elderly woman, Shelby Blair, came home to an intruder in her home. She was subsequently ambushed," the Coral Gables detective conveyed. "She fought him off and disarmed him, but not without sustaining injuries."

"How were the police notified?" Mansfield asked.

"You won't believe this, but the invader fled the scene on foot, perhaps to a waiting car. This elderly resident was out walking her dog, and when she got back, she entered through the front door and found the intruder. He came at her with some military-issued blade, the Labrador attacked, and Ms. Blair took the knife from him after a terrifying struggle. Once he ran, she called 911 and said she needed help."

"Did he take anything?" Mansfield asked.

"To be honest, I don't think he was able to. She came home too soon. He left a tool sack behind when he left. The bag contained a suspicious device, and the explosives team is now investigating."

"Gotcha, I'm almost at Freedom Pointe. Thanks for filling me in."

Mansfield arrived in time to watch the squad depart. He checked in with the crime scene coordinator and then found Danny D.

"So fake or real?"

"It looked like a pipe bomb. Cylinder-shaped, however, not explosive," the Grease detective responded with a shrug of the shoulders.

"What in the hell? So what's the purpose? Does it look random or targeted? Is someone trying to scare her?" Mansfield asked more of himself than anyone else. No one answered. He looked over the crime scene before picking up the retriever's leash and dog food bag and jogging up the street to Jackie's place.

Her door stood open before Dave knocked. He took stock of his mom, who looked frail for the first time in his life. Hoping it was his imagination playing tricks on him, he took off Sadie's collar and walked inside the cabin, hugging his mother.

"Well…" was the only word Jackie spoke when he let her go.

"An intruder broke into Bee's while she took the dog for a walk. When they came home, he assaulted her with a blade. The pup tried to protect her. Bee took the knife from the prowler but paid a heavy price for her bravery."

"Good for her," his mom spouted. "For a 76-year-old to stick up for herself, fantastic. Where did they take her? How is she?"

"They took her to Coral Gables Hospital. She sustained swollen eyes and some lacerations on her face and head. I looked around, and blood was around the cabin from a significant struggle. I called the emergency room, and they said she would be kept overnight."

Jackie laughed and sat down, relieved, "He messed with the wrong old lady! But Dave, this intrusion is still quite a shock because crime doesn't happen in this retirement community. What was this guy after?"

"Mom, we can only guess. It seems likely that the men watching Bee's house are connected to this. They wanted to leave a make-believe explosive device in her house to scare her, but she caught them in the act."

"What in the world are you talking about?" Jackie stood up in surprise. Dave explained about the tool kit containing the non-explosive bomb found in the kitchen.

"Mom, have you taken Caspar over to Bee's?"

"What an odd thing to ask! The answer is, of course, but only once, a couple of days ago. The stress of those guys hanging around outside got to her because one night, she said she didn't want to leave the cabin. So we picked up her dinner and brought it over to her. We sat with her while she ate. Why do you ask about him?"

"My gut says something is off about him. You must not sense this. Otherwise, you would not be hanging around with him. Did he ask any questions at Bee's about her or her unique collection of expensive Knick Knacks? Did he dismiss them as inexpensive?"

"Oh no, he took note. He gave the place the once over. He couldn't keep his hands off her pieces. Bee closed the doors to the back rooms to keep those items from view. Thomas removed some heirlooms over the past couple of months. I can't imagine what he would have done if all the antiques were still around. He might have had a coronary."

"Mom, this is what I'm talking about. Don't you think his actions are weird? The public doesn't understand the value of artifacts like those in Bee's house. They wouldn't anticipate seeing them in the home of an older woman. The location of the items should have caused him to reassess any thoughts he may have entertained of their worth. But he ignored all of that and instead assumed they were valuable. So many things about him don't add up."

"Are you sure you don't like him because he is my friend," Jackie asked with a smirk.

"No, Mom, did you tell him Bee gave you that first edition? Has he seen it?"

"For pity's sake, no! That thing is put away so no one can ever find it. I don't want anyone to know anything worth that much is in this house. I don't want to be the next target."

"Again, Jackie. Listen to yourself. This intruder must be tied to Thomas and the guys who pull his strings. Why else would Bee be targeted? Caspar verified that she indeed had the goods, and then two days later, the assault. I'm calling Peter."

Chapter 32

It was a crisp Monday morning, and Jade Holmes settled into her worn leather chair, the faint scent of coffee wafting from the mug on her cluttered desk. The hum of her computer filled the air as she dove into the next edition of the community scandal sheet. With its dog-eared pages and faded ink, *The Blood Line* served as the monthly underground communication vampires relied on to stay connected. With each turn of the page, the subtle rustle of paper echoed in the room, transporting Jade to a world of hidden secrets and unspoken truths.

Inside the pages of *The Blood Line*, Jade's words held power. The ink-stained paper absorbed her thoughts, giving them tangible form. Her editorials, written with a fiery passion, left a lasting mark on the reader's life force. The distinct scent of ink filled the room, its intense aroma a testament to the clandestine nature of the publication.

Now and then, a flicker of delight crossed Jade's face as she stumbled on a hidden gem—a comic strip bursting with vibrant colors, capturing fragments of vampire life with playfulness and charm. She couldn't help but chuckle at the clever punchlines, a brief respite from the seriousness that penetrated the scandal sheet.

Jade considered herself a finicky creature with moods that changed from content to upset within seconds. The ability to perceive her anger allowed her followers to understand when to back off and give her space instead of escalating the situation. She sat with her arms crisscrossed on her chest, tapping her crossed foot, and staring at the blank paper before her.

A week had passed since the blood bag Luca Medina hung around with lost half her head. She had been extra saucy to anyone daring to address her after the murder, and she had been praying that no one would connect the bitch to the covens. Then, this morning, a swan told her a detective showed up at Luca's house on Saturday. This news released a tsunami of involuntary memories.

Jade was born and raised in Germany, her childhood immersed in vast, marshy plains dissected by winding ditches and artificial canals. The distance between farms seemed endless. In the vicinity, a reclusive community dwelled, regarded with suspicion and perceived as threatening by the locals, their isolation fueling rumors and fear. Jade vividly recalled the tales that echoed through her upbringing, warning her against venturing into their territory, as no one had ever dared to bridge the divide and unravel their mysteries.

She recalled a night when her mom and the other 13 farmhands had returned from a hard day's labor, and all gathered in the house for some lively conversation before turning in. At the time, she was four years old and complained about having to go to bed at eight.

At some time during the night, her mother and grandfather reacted to loud sounds outside the house. Her mom placed her in a cedar chest and piled pillows on her while her grandfather went onto the porch. The prowlers forced him to rouse everyone in the house and collect them into one room after being threatened by firearms.

The invaders went through everything, including the container where Jade had been concealed. They passed the trunk by because they lacked interest in pillows. Everything else, however, the gang packed up, including clothing, valuables, jewelry, and kitchenware. Afterward, the men ordered everyone to the cellar.

While Jade had experienced a sense of unease during her confinement in the crate, it became a tangible fear gripping her tightly as she strained her ears to hear the faint sounds of the others descending into the basement depths. Every ounce of her little body yearned to voice protests, to unleash a decisive 'no' into the darkness. However, with the echoes of her mother's hushed instructions fresh in her mind, urging her to remain silent no matter what she overheard, she stuck her fist in her mouth. In her young imagination, the vivid image of the underground space materialized, its ceiling low, leaving no room for a grown-up to stand, intensifying her apprehension.

The robber with the deep voice and the other three went to the cellar because the house became very still. Until, crack, ting, pop, so loud she moved her hands to cover her ears. Another and another until she lost count, and tears drenched the fabric surrounding her. The men returned upstairs, loaded their spoils, and took off, taking her grandfather's truck.

After a long while had passed, Jade crawled out of the cedar chest and ran down to the cellar. Somehow, she understood the clan needed help, and she managed to reach the neighboring people, even if they were off-limits, 1.25 miles down the dirt path, by riding her bicycle with the training wheels attached the entire way. That night she lost her whole family but also found a new one. The vampire community next door took her in and raised her until she became old enough to leave for Buffalo, New York.

The police rounded up three of the four intruders. They were Polish and confessed to being killers of the immortal bloodsuckers. They called themselves slayers. The problem was that nobody in the region believed in vampires. The German community executed them all as uneducated robbers and murderers.

Jade tried to concentrate on her article, but her mind seethed with these memories. She wanted to destroy something, protect the coven, and get off her ass. With a jolt, she came out of her musings. A young boy entered and told her two men came to the door asking to speak with her.

"Damn it," Jade shouted to the boy, who looked like he might faint or wet his trousers. She walked in a circle, balled up her fists, and clenched her jaws. She picked up the lamp on her desk and threw the ugly thing against the wall. The young boy took off in the opposite direction, darted down the catwalk that ran the length of the house, and found safety far from the angry master.

Gathering herself, she walked downstairs and into the sitting room where the detectives waited. Her blood-red pursed lips and big bouffant-styled black hair did not discourage the immediate eye contact and powerful connection between her and the blonde one. Mansfield had been told a mutual gaze might lead to an attraction, but he was also sure that would not happen here.

This meeting was simple: non-romantic, non-sexual curiosity. He intended to figure her out. He looked at her because he did not like what was in front of him. He glanced over at Landers, who looked in every direction except that of Ms. Holmes.

After an awkward moment where the parties sized each other up, Mansfield slipped into a routine and made introductions, indicating they wanted to talk to her about the Moody triple homicide. Jade stood still, staring at the men. She did not offer them a seat and did not reply.

The detective continued, "Ms. Holmes, since your name came up twice during the investigation, we figured it would be wise to speak with you and ask if you could add anything."

"Nice cologne. Must you marinate in it?" Jade stated while she took a seat in a magnificent antique-looking chair. The detectives took her hint and sat across her on a hard, seldom-used sofa. Mansfield thought it best to let the comment go by without a response.

"Ms. Holmes, what is your association with Victoria Moody?" The more seasoned detective went straight to the topic at hand. He had no desire to tiptoe around with this woman and try to make her comfortable.

"None. I have no relationship. I don't even know her."

"Would you say you had a cordial rapport with the deceased?" He kept pushing forward, ignoring her resistance. The room went silent, and everyone sat quietly except Landers, who continued to tap his pen on the clean sheet in his notebook.

"Jesse," Jade's voice carried with immense power toward the open door, "Would you please bring us a pitcher of iced tea and three glasses of ice." The room returned to silence.

"How well acquainted are you and Victoria Moody, Ms. Holmes?" Mansfield asked again, pretending she had not noticed the question the first time.

"Are you simpleminded?" Jade snapped. "I just told you I did not know her. Never had dealings with her. My sons went to middle school with her." Dave drew in a deep breath and practiced the six-second pause. That, or her expression, would reveal real suffering.

"So why did she write about you on her blog? Why was she afraid of you?"

"How am I supposed to understand what a teenager does or thinks? Luca may have told her fibs. I'm sorry I hurt your feelings when I called you an idiot. I honestly assumed you knew."

"Why would Luca tell stories about you to her?" Landers interjected, giving Mansfield time to collect himself.

"Who can say why that charlatan does the things he does? Everyone is normal until you begin to understand them."

"Luca said he and Vicki ran into you and your two boys while shopping, and you behaved pretty nasty to her. He also explained the connection between you and him as not great," Landers offered. He leaned forward toward Jade, his elbows on his knees, rubbing his hands together.

"He said you consider the relationship to be adversarial. You and Luca come from different regions of the United States, and this causes some friction. But beyond this, you have a common enemy, serial killers who refer to themselves as slayers." As this last comment was being conveyed, Jesse entered the room and deposited the drinks as requested. Without saying a word or acknowledging anyone, he fled quickly.

Mansfield filled his glass with tea and poured a second. The curtains at the window stirred with ancient pain. Both detectives waited for a response from the obnoxious woman. She had been making several facial comments throughout Landers' remarks, so he did not hope for much.

"Oops! Did I just roll my eyes out loud?" With her fangs almost protruding, Jade remarked with an open-lipped smile. "I need to teach my 'fuck you' face how to use its inside voice."

Dave stood and paced around the room, looking at the antiquities. "What is your relationship with Luca Medina? I want to make a note of your side."

"Luca is nothing but a kid trying to fill shoes too big for him. He must gain the experience, understanding, and maturity to be a leader. This group has been here long before he dropped out of school, and we have been well-established and safe, with a straight connection to Buffalo."

"Now the New Orleans clan decided to move into town, and they put this… this toddler in charge. This guy can end up being responsible for our deaths. I have been through such a thing: the annihilation of a group of people, of a family. I find nothing worse than being the only survivor of something of this magnitude."

Stunned at the emotion they had witnessed, the detectives became aware that Ms. Holmes now wanted to chop her head off for losing control in front of them. But the things she said did confirm, in a roundabout way, the things Luca talked about.

"Jade, what do you do for a living?" Mansfield asked, changing the subject.

"Mr. Curly Hair, I found your nose. It was in my business. The shit you read about me is not true. I am much worse. Best you don't forget that. Time for you to leave."

"Do you have an alibi for the time of the murders?" Landers asked as he stood.

"At a prayer meeting. Ask anyone around here."

As they walked to the front door, Mansfield asked if she owned any firearms or other weapons. She laughed and said she did not need them. Landers asked one last question about whether she knew anybody who would have wanted to hurt Victoria Moody. Jade Holmes slammed the door without answering.

Chapter 33

"Well, that was different," Landers said as his partner started the car.

"Yeah, well, we experienced enough opposition to derail a train. Therefore, we succeeded admirably. I'm not sure about you, but I resisted the impulse to be aggressive and switched to active listening. We learned some useful nuggets," Dave replied. "I don't think she killed the Moody's, but I do think she is terrified the murder might lead back to her, and she could be the next fatality."

"Do you think there is another victim?"

"No, I don't. But she thinks there might be." Mansfield turned onto SW 67th Avenue. "The drive to Bluestockings is a good time to catch up since we have the better part of an hour. Can you believe that is the name of the real estate agency Jake Mendoza owns? Where do these people dream up these names? We are going all the way over to Coconut Grove."

"Yeppers. He's the guy married to that middle school principal who was having a relationship with Evie Moody. Gotcha. It is about time we got around to him." Landers opened the file and flipped through the data the various search engines mined.

"Let's see, if he was aware, we know that the affair with his wife had given him reason to resent Ms. Moody. Also, remember when we interviewed Ms. Mendoza, she said she would provide us with information from the security company. I am not surprised she never did."

"I got tired of waiting, so I followed up, and we have it for October. The logs show her locking down the house around 9:30 when she says she went to bed. The following log was Jake's code, unlocking the door to come home at 11:10."

Mansfield grabbed a toothpick from the car console and stuck it between his front teeth. He immediately removed the pick and threw it out the window as memories of his tooth surfaced. "That doesn't exactly give the principal an alibi, but it takes some suspicion off her as a primary. But Jake just climbed up a rung on the ladder of doubt."

Landers continued, "Mr. Mendoza also harbors a professional reason to resent Evie because they were competitors in the Miami real estate market. As research showed, they keep battling each other on some big deals. He wins some, and she scores some, but he is a sore loser. He won many awards for sales over the years, both residential and commercial, and was recognized for all sorts of deeds within the community."

"In May 2004, he was a finalist for the Distinguished Service Award from the National Association of Realtors. In 2003, he was also nominated but did not win the Realtor of the Year title. Public records show he owns a registered gun and a pistol, but nothing about a shotgun."

"Humm," Mansfield rubbed his chin while he thought for a minute. "Can you find out who won last year and this year?"

"Does a bear shit?" Landers responded. He reached for the phone and called Erik Green at the station's front desk.

Mansfield's phone rang. "Hello, Peter. Glad you called me back."

"Sorry, it took me so long. Things are popping around here today."

"I bet. Have you been filled in on the break-in at Shelby Blair's house yesterday?"

"Yep. She is one of the things on the front of the stove. I'm not sure what all that with the fake bomb was about, but beating up an old lady isn't cool." Peter sounded winded.

"Where are you? You sound like you just ran a marathon."

"Close, maybe a 10k. It looks like those goons who were watching Ms. Blair might be gone. Thomas has disappeared for now. We are getting too close, and people are nervous," Peter said.

"Well, on the one hand, that's good news. How do we ensure his mother is safe?"

"A man is authorized to guard the house once she goes home until things calm. Someone is with her at the hospital. We hope Thomas tries to go to his mom's, and we need to ensure the goon squad doesn't show up again."

"Great. Peter, thanks for the update." Mansfield hung up the phone and looked at his partner, who was staring back at him.

"Trouble with a friend of Jackie's. Someone broke into her cabin yesterday and beat her up. Her son is mixed up with some bad people, and they let their anger out on his mom. I promised Jackie I would investigate," Mansfield explained. "Anything on Mendoza yet?"

"Of course." Landers smiled. "The Realtor of the Year for Florida in 2003 was the beautiful Evie Moody. And, if that isn't a coincidence, she also earned the Distinguished Service Award."

"Now, ain't that some shit!" the detective snickered. "For a man who doesn't like to lose, it sounds like she was a large, sharp pain in Mr. Mendoza's ass."

Mansfield checked his wristwatch. There was about 40 minutes left in the drive. "Are we still on for the update with Johns this afternoon?"

"Unfortunately, we are," Landers complained. "We better make sure we have our shit together this time, or we are back to patrol."

"Sometimes, I just want to tell her to cancel my subscription because I don't need her issues. I have enough of my own." Mike roared into laughter, and Dave let a smile escape his usually serious face.

"All right, fill me in on what you found out on the follow-up with Gray," Mansfield said, bringing a light moment to an abrupt end.

"Ole, Charlie. He has not been candid with us. His name and social track back to a missing person from northern California. The original Charles Gray disappeared years ago while abroad on vacation. Then our Charlie reappeared in 1987, using this SSN, looking much younger and darker in Buffalo."

"It sounds like someone helped our man by forging papers and a passport with the missing person's social security number. I couldn't find anything on him before he appeared in New York, where he was until he came to Miami. The rest of the story, you know."

"Buffalo? Did you say Buffalo? What a coincidence. Didn't Jade Holmes rant about a safe connection straight to Buffalo? Landers, do you believe in coincidences?" his partner asked sarcastically.

"This is a point to follow up on. I thought about the magnet on the refrigerator at Moody's place. So I gave the place another call to ask if Mr. Gray was a member instead of Mr. Moody. Bingo! Not only does he belong, but he holds three championship titles. I talked to the owner, who described Charles as arrogant but proficient with firearms. His marksmanship is excellent, and he usually stores his pieces in his locker at the club."

"I thought he told us he didn't own any guns?" Mansfield said.

"He sure did, so I pulled the gun registrations, and he owns two registered. No shotguns, though. The last point relates to the name he gave you, 'Suflet Intunecat'. This took two seconds to decode on the Internet. The words are Romanian and translated to mean *Dark Soul*."

"The hell you say?" Mansfield glanced over at Landers with his sharp, penetrating eyes.

"Yes, Romanian. Why are you so surprised?"

"On Saturday, when Slater and I interviewed him, I told her I thought he had a Slovak accent. I was thinking of Slovakia, the Czech Republic, or Hungary, but Romania also fits."

"What? Did you guys get the impression he was from one of these areas or immigrated from one?"

"Precisely. So, if you did not find background on him before 1987, this makes me wonder what was going on in Romania in that year and the previous 15 years or so. See if that computer can tell us while I drive." Landers put in another call to Erik. A half-hour later, he announced he was ready.

"Good thing," Mansfield answered. "Only about 10 minutes until we arrive. Took your sweet time, didn't you?"

"This is incredible. I should have been a history major. Here's Romania, the cliff notes version, anyway. Nicolae Ceausescu seized power in 1965 and created a de facto communist dictatorship that ruled until the end of the revolution in 1989. In the late sixties, his government issued a decree prohibiting contraception and abortion. Romanian women suffered the worst. Children taken from their parents were raised in state orphanages."

"The ones the government considered damaged or defective were separated. These outcasts were hidden in remote facilities like the southern Carpathian mountains, the village of Comanesti near Asau, and the mountaintops surrounding the town of Bran in the district of Transylvania. I'm sure there are more places, but these few make the point. To be Black was to be considered irreparably flawed. The Romanian people had an underground market that transported books, movies, films, and people."

"Sounds like Charles was a good candidate to be smuggled out."

"Yes indeed. He would have been close to Vlad the Impaler's castle if he had been in the orphanage near Transylvania. In case you don't recall... he is considered their head vampire."

"Shut the hell up. Are you kidding me? You are actually drawing a connection here."

"Hey, I only follow the leads. Vampires and Charles are located in Romania; vamps, Charles, and Jade are in Buffalo; and the last touch, Holmes and Gray are in Miami." Landers couldn't hold back his laughter.

Chapter 34

Bluestockings was arrogant in its existence. The building catered to the aristocracy at the expense of commoners, making it lavish and ostentatious. For the average, hardworking Miami resident, the structure spat volumes. Everything about it screamed, "*I'm superior to you!*" from every blade of grass to every beveled mirror.

When walking on the flat, polished sidewalks surrounded by four-inch trimmed lush green lawns, the premises bellowed, "*Do not look at me like that. Do you think you can even try? I can tell by comparing your clothes to mine, shoes, hair, and car. You are trash and do not belong in this community. Stop sniveling and crawl back into whatever dumpster of a dwelling you came from.*"

The detectives parked in the designated lot and stood to take in the monstrosity for a minute. "You understand, Landers, although the establishment adds to the chemistry of the Grove, it assaults my humanity. Not that I want anything from the arrogant, pretentious people it calls to; it's just the sense of entitlement," Mansfield scoffed.

With a light laugh, Landers remarked, "Without a doubt, this isn't Evie Moody's way of doing business."

"No, it isn't. Though we have not met yet, I understand why she and Mendoza had been at odds," Dave replied.

Mansfield approached the receptionist, who looked familiar. He tried not to stare but was sure he had seen this woman somewhere before. "Hello, we are detectives with the Miami Police Department, and we are here to visit Mr. Mendoza. Can you advise him we are here?"

"Yes, please take a seat. You are scheduled."

Mansfield sat next to Landers, leaned over, and whispered if he recognized the woman at the desk. Mike looked up at her and admitted she did look a bit familiar, but he couldn't place her.

"There's a good chance she holds the key to everything, but we can't place her. Simply great!" his partner taunted.

A few minutes later, the detectives walked to Mendoza's office. At first glance, Mansfield thought the room was enormous. Jake might need to pack lunch to cross the football field between his desk and the door, where he should have been standing to shake their hands. Pictures and memorabilia of the realtor and other prominent town members were scattered haphazardly throughout the room, capturing them in diverse activities. A sweeping gaze across the space revealed a visual chronicle, offering insights into this man's identities, actions, and connections.

"Mr. Mendoza, I am Detective Mansfield, and this is my partner, Detective Landers. As I mentioned on the phone, we are working on the Moody triple homicide and need to verify some information with you if possible. We appreciate your time and cooperation," the lead investigator began.

Jake offered them a chair at the round table next to his library corner, and he also took a seat. "Always happy to help the police do their job," he said dryly.

"Thank you. Your marriage to Lee has lasted many years; she's the middle school principal where Cooper Moody studied. According to our research, she was an intimate friend of Evie Moody, one of your main competitors. Are these statements true?" Mansfield asked.

"Yes." Jake didn't bother to look up; his gaze fixed on the grain of the wooden pipe he had picked up, its polished surface catching the dim light over the table. He deliberately tamped the tobacco into the pipe bowl, feeling the gentle resistance beneath his fingertips. Ignoring the detective's presence, he focused on the rhythmic ritual, seeking solace in the familiarity of the task.

The investigator leaned forward, his voice cutting through the air. "Can you describe your activities on the evening of October 19?" Mansfield asked. Landers left the table and started canvassing the office.

The harsh scent of the freshly packed tobacco drifted around Jake as he drew in a deep breath, exhaling a plume of smoke that rose lazily toward the ceiling. The coils of smoke intertwined with the hazy atmosphere, casting a veil over the room. Jake's eyes remained fixed on the pipe, its stem clutched between his teeth, as he examined the detective's question.

"What does it matter? Am I a suspect?" Jake's voice was laced with indifference, a subtle defiance brewing beneath the surface.

"At this point, Mr. Mendoza, we are only gathering information. Can you please answer the question?" Landers interjected, his frustration palpable.

Jake remained still and again did not appear to be listening. A curl of blue smoke gracefully escaped the confines of the pipe bowl. It danced and swirled in the air, casting fleeting shadows against the worn pages of old case files on the bookshelf behind him. The smoke represented the unanswered questions in the room, lingering like a mystery waiting to be resolved.

"In many of these photos, you are hunting. Do you belong to a gun association? I was talking to someone the other day, and they told me the Miami Gun Club was the best, and I should investigate it." Landers decided to try a different tactic.

Mendoza almost laughed aloud. Instead, a big smile replaced the pipe at his lips. "Well, you received good advice. The club is the finest, most exclusive, and most expensive. I doubt you could afford it on a civil servant's pay."

"Well, this is good news because I am not a bureaucrat; I am considered a public servant," Landers said.

Jake Mendoza sat still and tried to size up Landers with a stare. He deepened his voice and let out his signature metallic laugh. "I appreciate that you are into gamesmanship. However, I would not go in that direction with me. Evie liked to do that, and look where she ended up."

"Did she end up dead because she offended you?" Mansfield asked bluntly.

"Now, you are putting words in my mouth. I was with a client on Tuesday evening. Trying to close a deal," the realtor offered.

"Are you acquainted with someone named Charles Gray?" Landers gambled while he was looking at the hunting pictures.

"Why do you ask? Is he a suspect or something?" Jake responded.

"He is also a member of the Miami Gun Club, and I thought maybe you guys had bumped into each other." Mansfield monitored how Landers and Mendoza interacted with one another. The last question hit close to home.

"I do not believe so. But many members belong that I don't associate with," Jake grunted.

"This is an interesting picture. It looks old," Landers said. "Is this your father and you as a younger man?"

"Yes. One of my most vivid memories of him was going out to the cabin and hunting with the old shotgun he had. He taught me most of what I know about the woods."

Mansfield lit up and sat forward, directing his words to the realtor. "2002?"

"Excuse me, what?"

"Your receptionist, she's from 2002. Was it January or February?" Landers looked at the two men, lost. The conversation took a turn somewhere while he looked at the hunting pictures.

Jake sat back in his chair, and his defenses cracked for a moment, and he became the personable realtor his customers dealt with. "Hey, you're right. February. How did you recognize her? I found her about six months ago. She cost a lot but is worth every cent. The clients go wild when they figure out who she is."

"I give. What are you guys talking about?" Mike asked at last.

"Remember, I told you the receptionist looked familiar, and you said she did also. It came to me at once. She was the bunny of the month in the February 2002 issue. It had been bugging me, and at last, it came to me," Mansfield explained, as he had just won an Emmy. Landers shook his head. What a thing to bond over.

"Jake, if you are not acquainted with Charles Gray, you should at least recognize his name because he holds three championship titles for the club," Landers stated. The business side of Jake returned as fast as it had left. He took a long drag on the pipe and did not respond.

"Mr. Mendoza, we need the names of the customers you entertained on Tuesday evening. We need to demonstrate your movements from six o'clock until you activated the home alarm at 11:10. If you could get this to us by tomorrow, it would be great. This way, we can rule you out," Mansfield stated.

"The hell you say. I thought I was not a suspect."

"We questioned you to establish an alibi for your wife; however, you were not at your house until after the killings. So she can't account for your whereabouts, and you cannot explain her situation. We must check out your activities," Landers explained.

"Mr. Mendoza, do you own any firearms?" Mansfield asked.

"Yes. It is registered and in my locker at the club."

"What about a shotgun? The registrations include no mention of this type of weapon."

"Well, I guess I don't own one," he said sarcastically.

"One last question, how is Lee holding up since the murders? Is she considering filing for divorce yet?" As the investigator pushed, Jake was almost ejected from his sitting chair; his reaction was too forceful. His bottom half was caught, or he would have soared across the space between him and Mansfield.

"She's having a rough time now and does not recognize what she wants. Leave her alone." Jake threatened.

The detectives shook their heads. They got what they came for. Now it was time to go.

Chapter 35

Morgan Johns requested an update, and Mansfield and Landers worked to put it together. With the day almost gone, they wanted to enter and leave as fast as possible. Their strategy was to bring her up to speed while avoiding her inevitable anger and sarcastic responses to the report.

The sergeant often began by attempting to place everyone at ease, reminding them they all worked toward the same goals and should maintain a sense of camaraderie. By demonstrating shared values with her investigators, she hoped to encourage more candid conversations. However, the detectives would experience the pressure of the sergeant's demands and often find themselves at a juncture of 'fight, flight, or freeze'.

They decided to present the case with two potential possibilities. One, the burglar shot the family all on his own, a burglary gone wrong. Two, a hired killer performed the murders and took the mugs as a cover-up.

Mansfield explained, "Option One appeared less likely than Option Two because the thief came and left without many valuables. It doesn't make sense to kill three people over three beer steins. A true robber would have taken more of the antiques." Landers sat next to his partner and nodded his head in agreement.

"Tell me more about the second choice," Johns encouraged.

"We've been working with six potential suspects," Dave started.

"Six! Where the hell did all these people come from? Who are they?"

Mansfield detected the familiar anger in his chest. Sometimes he wished he were an octopus, enabling him to slap her eight times and order her to be quiet until he finished. Instead, he employed a simple anchoring technique he had learned to calm his body and signal to his brain that he was not in immediate physical danger.

He thought about his feet and wiggled his toes. He put his shoes firmly on the ground, alerting his appendages and heels that they were secure and prompting him to remember to exhale fully before beginning his next breath. This gave him time to think about what to say or do next. He had to do this because the six-second rule simply did not work with his sergeant.

Landers stood and paced the room, saying, "Sarge, it doesn't matter where they came from. The investigation led us to them. Three of them have confirmed alibis, and the other three gave us their whereabouts, but we have yet to be able to track them down. We found a shotgun in the workplace of Charles Gray, Mark Moody's lover, but we cannot tie the firearm to him because of the unlimited access to its storage place."

"We can prove that Jake Mendoza, whose wife had an affair with Evie Moody, is acquainted with Charles, even though he denies the fact. In addition, Jake was a professional competitor of Evie in the real estate world, and he does not take losing very well."

"Jade Holmes and Luca Medina, Victoria Moody's boyfriend, maintain an unhealthy relationship, and all three are into the vampire culture. They are afraid of slayers killing off anyone associated with the covens."

Morgan sat in her chair, shaking her head back and forth. Dave predicted her temper flare was only seconds away. The vampires would be the outrageousness she would not endure. Everything happened in slow motion. She was ready to detonate when Mansfield's phone rang. He looked down, and Sandra's number popped up.

Mansfield jumped up like he was taking the jump shot to win the game and bounced. Landers' eyes followed him as he exited the room, and Johns closed her mouth immediately. Landers noticed the sound of her teeth hitting each other as her jaw shut with some force.

"Now, where does he think he's going?" the sergeant said in an almost normal voice.

"I... I don't... I don't have any... The call must be important," Landers replied as he sat.

Within an abbreviated time, Mansfield reentered the office and announced that the medical examiner had some results on the DNA. They needed to get to her fast. This might be the needed break. Johns dismissed them, and they ran out of the building.

It took 10 minutes to drive the two miles to the Miami-Dade county medical examiner's office, where she waited. When the detectives arrived, they expected the usual mini-lecture before receiving the results. Sandra thought the only way for police officers to have a proper education in the basics was for her to teach them.

She began, "DNA is most often used to solve crimes in one of two ways," then she stopped talking and looked at the two men. "But you don't need me to go over this now." Mansfield appreciated not having to sit through another lecture.

"Thank you. What exactly did you find?" Landers tried to spur her along.

"Well, I had to call in some major favors. I want to make sure you guys realize this came at a cost. This guy's sheet isn't much. He got popped in the early nineties for breaking and entering but has been clean since. Remarkable, really."

"Good. Name and address, please."

"Fine. All right. The name is Robert Price, 62, and the location is NW 29th St, Miami." Dave reached over, took the paper she offered, and kissed her on the cheek as he and his partner bolted.

"This is in Allapattah. A rough neighborhood," Mansfield said as they approached the sedan. Landers called in for backup. They didn't know what they would encounter. Moving steel weighed down the streets with its stench and pollution. It took them 15 minutes to drive to the area, which was only three to five miles away. Mansfield hated rush hour.

The officers rolled up on a crumbling property, and the detectives arrived within seconds of the squad cars. The dilapidated carport no longer protected vehicles from the elements as it struggled to remain erect. Nothing was visible from the road. If uprooted and planted elsewhere, the house would be an eyesore, but it fit right in here, on this street.

Landers looked through the windows. "Nothing appears maniacal," he announced. The police officers took the back while the investigators knocked on the front door. No answer.

The radio squawked. "Hey Dave, we found a vehicle back here, covered with a tarp. Underneath the cover is a dark-colored Nissan Maxima. It looks to be one of the newer models."

"This is the guy. Witnesses reported a car matching this description at the scene on the night of the murders. We're breaching."

Before busting down the door, Landers checked the doorknob. To everyone's surprise, he found an unlocked door. Mansfield and Landers cleared the house and told the patrol officers they would come out the back door.

A thorough search of the house turned up nothing related to the crime. No weapons or stolen items were located. The only thing tying this man to the homicides was his DNA on the stairway and in his car.

However, it appeared that someone had been staying with Mr. Price. They slept on the couch, as shown by the presence of a pillow and a stack of folded blankets. Dirty dishes for two were also left in the sink. Mansfield mused, did he read things all wrong? Did he have two intruders on his hands? He had dismissed this complication, but now it might be all too possible.

The forensic team gathered data from the car. The passenger seat contained blood, and two fingerprint sets could be positively identified. The Nissan remained in the backyard because the detectives thought Price might return soon because of the unlocked front door. After installing the monitoring equipment, everyone departed the premises. Dave and Mike settled into an easy silence.

Most detectives avoided surveillance jobs at all costs, but Mansfield had never minded stakeouts in all his years on the job. He often enjoyed them because they allowed him to analyze his cases from different angles. When they were active, there was little time to step back and reflect, and there was no shortage of information, none of which was particularly timely. The caveat was the partner, which meant someone who did not talk for the sake of talking. Landers was the right company, even though he bellyached about stakeouts to other officers.

Chapter 36

For Bobby's safety, he had to leave the house. He suffered from cabin fever and boredom. It had been almost a week since the murders, and Archer insinuated that he was tense and irritable. He became worried that if he didn't do something soon, he would lose control and roll about the floor, shouting profanities.

With his survival teetering on his sanity, Bobby convinced himself the police wouldn't be looking for two elderly gentlemen, so they should be safe if they went out for a while and didn't call attention to themselves. They went to the city's historic core and rode into downtown Miami, home of one of the area's most notable attractions. Always a treat.

An afternoon on the town for this unique pair meant hot dogs served in various fanciful arrangements. Jumping into Archer's truck, the younger man drove them to the Dogma, a chic little eatery on a stretch of Biscayne Boulevard. The music in the kitchen was quiet, the servers were in their twenties, and there were a few small tables close to the counter.

Bobby ordered the healthy Athens Dog with cucumbers, tomatoes, onions, olives, and feta cheese. Archer, alternatively, chose the rich Pomodoro, which had bruschetta and feta cheese on top. Walking out of the place, rubbing their bellies like a pair of pregnant women, both men paused to take in the historic heart of Miami, the site of early 20th-century urban development and Miami's birthplace. It was October, during the shoulder season, when the weather was mild and the crowds were thin.

Archer and his younger friend strolled around Bayfront Park, where a bronze statue of Christopher Columbus stood since 1952. The benches around the Italian explorer provided a wonderful place to sit while digestion did its work. The grounds were peaceful, still green, and welcoming. Bobby was happy to be able to live in South Florida and thought he was a lucky man. The non-refrigerated fresh air was energizing, and he began to relax as no furtive glances were coming their way since leaving the house.

On the way home, the old truck puffed as the Boulevard became clogged with clamoring motorists. Bobby flipped on the car radio, and the story of the hour announced that law enforcement had a break in the Angel Bluff murder investigation. He almost wrecked the vehicle by pulling over to listen to the broadcast.

"According to police sources, DNA testing of evidence found at the scene led to identifying a suspect. The alleged perpetrator, Robert Price, is a 62-year-old senior living near Allapattah. On the night of the killings, witnesses saw Price's car parked in front of the victim's house. It was later located at his home. He is considered armed and dangerous. Anyone with information relating to the whereabouts of Mr. Price should steer clear and contact the police at once," the radio announced with all the authority of god.

Bobby changed positions in his seat and looked at his friend, speechless. After seconds passed, he said, "I had an inkling this day would come, but I never thought it would. A search is underway to find me. Why now?"

"Because you left evidence behind," Archer replied. "I don't see why you didn't wait until you got outdoors, where the rain would clean everything up." Bobby turned around in the truck seat while banging his fists on the steering wheel. What a week, and never once had he planned his moves if this situation occurred.

"How stupid can I be?" He said while rubbing his face with both of his hands. "I bet there is surveillance set up at my house."

"Agreed. Let's go to my place and figure something out," Archer said, making sense for the first time. "Do you want me to drive?"

Pulling back into traffic, he responded, "No, I got it."

Praying the connection had not been made yet, the two older gents headed to Archer's home while the homicide detectives waited for them at Bobby's residence. Mansfield's phone rang, and looking at the screen, told him Johns was calling. He took a deep breath and answered.

"Morgan. Do you need us? Everything is quiet here," Mansfield said, wondering why she called.

"Bad news, boys," the sergeant responded, sounding beaten and abnormal. Dave sat up straighter in his seat and glanced over at Landers, snapping his fingers to bring him to attention, causing Mike to tense. Ensuring his partner could listen, he pressed the speaker button.

"I updated the LT on the DNA and what you uncovered at Price's house. Instead of saying 'good job' and moving on, he held a press conference and gave the vultures everything. I was in awe and found myself speechless. I tell you what, good judgment is like deodorant; the people who need it most never use it."

"He told me directly, and I quote, 'The mass media beast maintains an insatiable appetite, and no public agency, much less the police, can afford to starve it entirely. We found this lead, so we can find others.' We exchanged words, but the result is that Mr. Robert Price's photo and credentials are being circulated in the media. He wouldn't set foot anywhere near his domicile if he is smart."

"Fuck me to tears!" Mansfield thundered. Without warning, he sensed a sharp pain in his head that peaked and went away like the fog of a scary lake. "Relax, I think I figured something out," and he hung up the phone with this statement.

On the way to the science lab, Dave filled Mike in on his plan, and they turned on the radio. The breaking news interrupted the daily broadcast three times during the 40-minute trip to Doral, where the Forensic Services Bureau was. When the detectives reached the FSB building, nine o'clock approached, and streetlights lit up the parking lot. Mansfield entered the LT's badge number to open the front glass doors that remained locked after sunset. He shouldn't have had the digits, but he did, so what the hell?

When the investigators saw the security officer making his rounds, they made a beeline for the elevators. The car stank like stale breath and body odor from a day of customary law and order in an institution. Landers pushed the button marked three, the floor that housed the Fingerprint Identification Unit. The secretary had left hours ago, allowing the detective to lean over the countertop and press the switch, which buzzed the glass door open and permitted access to the back rooms. Sol Osiel was still working, sitting at his desk.

"How'd you break in here?"

"We let ourselves in."

"Mansfield, don't tell me that. You can't go around breaching security." Dave nodded in remorse.

"What do you want?" Sol asked.

"Robert Price, connected to the Moody triple homicide." Landers pulled a second chair away from another desk, and the detectives took a seat. Only the three sat in the lab office, but Mansfield spoke low and conspiratorially, hoping to draw the FI tech into the immediacy of what he was about to say.

"Did you catch this afternoon's broadcast?" Mansfield half-whispered.

"No, some of us need to work. What do you want?"

"Well, a statement said our number one suspect is Price. LT leaked the info, and they are discussing the particulars all over the news. After realizing he wouldn't go near his residence any time soon, we ceased our observation. We left some patrol officers but had to go to the next play. Any idea what this might be?"

"Anything to do with why you are over here this time of night?"

"Give the man a star," Landers clapped. "We need the ID on those prints you picked up in the car earlier. Got to find Price before he goes too far under."

"Why didn't you guys call instead of driving over here? I could be home now."

"Would you have answered the phone?"

"No." Sol grinned. "As it happens, you are in luck. I just finished a match-up and got a nine-point match. I intended to complete the report before I left." The investigators knew that fingerprints only needed to pair up in five places to be used in court as proof of identification. This was too good.

"Damn, Osiel, this is almost as good as having a photo of the person inside Moody's house standing over the corpse. Don't hold back; give us the good news," Mansfield said with animation.

"Of course, they belong to one Mr. Archer Cohen, 81. The last address on file is NW 32nd Street." Sol handed over the paper with the information.

"One more thing before we leave. I wanted to ensure you got the shotgun we picked up from the firehouse," Mansfield asked.

"Yeppers sure did. Why?"

"Well, did you lift anything? Fingerprints, blood, or anything that would tie the damned thing to the crime scene?"

"No prints, but some blood on the butt. We took samples and submitted them for matching to the victims, but they returned negative. I don't have the ballistics report yet."

"What if I found another person to match the specimens to? Can you do this quickly? If I send a name, maybe a fluid sample or something like that?"

"Yeah. Depending on what you have."

Chapter 37

Even though the Dolphin Expressway was busy, travel time was shorter than on the way to Doral. Cohen's address was a few blocks from Robert Price's, so the detectives looped back to Allapattah. The investigators could tell from the writing style on the gang graffiti that many of the neighborhood residents were Latino.

Without any outside sources of light, the double-wide hid in the shadows. The aluminum-roofed carport adjacent to the trailer was home to an ancient truck. Mansfield strained to listen to the music in the distance, but it soon disappeared when a plane flew overhead, headed for the nearby international airport.

Because the investigators didn't know what they might find, Landers called for backup, and two MPD vehicles were already there. Officers set a perimeter around the mobile home while the detectives went to the door. Mansfield declared by knocking and announcing the police presence without response. As his partner kicked in the front door, he radioed the agents in the back to the breach. The door yielded so effortlessly that Landers almost crashed through. The officers cleared the trailer in a matter of minutes.

"No one is here," a young patrol officer announced, lowering his weapon. This last statement hung like fog, and the detectives tried to ignore it.

"Look around. Find what you can find." Mansfield gave the order after taking his time to look over and orient himself to the space. The place smelled like old sweat, worry, and hopelessness, reminding him of the holding cells.

Dave walked to the kitchen sink, sparkling clean, and leaned back against the countertop to brood. His eyes, as sharp as bullets, touched every surface within his range of vision. Archer Cohen must have been staying elsewhere since he had not been here for a while. No dishes, no trash, and a few aged groceries.

Landers' disappointment became evident as he sauntered off to look for weapons. Both detectives went outside to check the grounds. Once the MPD cleared the backyard shed, no part of the property had been missed.

"My internal system says the clock must be approaching 11:00. These guys aren't youngsters, and it's too late for them. Where would they be if not at Price's house and not here?" Landers asked in frustration. He didn't expect an answer.

Mansfield thanked the team for the backup and accompanied them to the street. He turned to look at the weather-beaten dwelling and, as a last thought, asked, "Hey, did any of you guys check out the truck?" The general response was no. One crew thought the other had it covered.

"Ah, can you wait a minute while we clear this one last area?" the detective asked as he grabbed his partner and headed for the vehicle with his flashlight. One sweep of the bright light into the cab eliminated it as a foxhole. When Landers looked in the truck's bed, he discovered the usual assortment of tools and items concealed by a tarp. He pulled off the canvas and saw two old people hiding in sleeping bags. His partner shined the flashlight in their direction.

"Would you, by any chance, be Mr. Price and Mr. Cohen?" Mansfield asked as both men tried in desperation to raise their hands. Each stammered a response. MPD placed Bobby in one cruiser and Archer in another and transported them downtown. The detectives followed.

"To be honest, I can't put my finger on what I was expecting, but that was not it," Landers said with a grin.

Mansfield laughed aloud and replied, "We should have suspected something was up by their ages, but to tell the truth, I expected a little more resistance myself."

The cold and sore men were given separate interview rooms. Archer walked into an eight-by-eight room where a small, cigarette-scarred table and three chairs awaited him. A handwritten sign on the wall said, "Pardon me, but you've mistaken me for someone who gives a damn!" Cohen waited for the investigators to arrive after being told to sit in the plastic chair.

Bobby walked into a room with a different setup. His encouragement on the wall said, "If the charge is homicide, not having done it before isn't an excuse for allowing bail!"

Mansfield sat Price down in a Slider—a wooden chair with the front two legs shortened and the seat waxed, causing a barely noticeable slope toward the table. These modifications caused him to continue sliding off the chair's front. The more he tried to sit back, the more he would slide toward the table. The dance ended with the suspect leaning forward, right into the faces of the detectives talking to him. Their first win.

Mansfield and Landers took seats in the two remaining chairs. The lead detective plopped one thick and one thin file before him. Both investigators sat in the quiet room for a minute or two, sizing up their opponent in this catch-the-mouse game they were about to play.

"Let's have a look, Mr. Robert Price. The case document says your friends call you Bobby. May I use this name?" Mansfield began.

"Oh, yes, sir. Everyone calls me Bobby."

"It says here you were a tradesman. In what industry did you work?" the detective asked, opening the thinner of the two files.

"I worked in the factory where we made yarn, thread, and fabric. Over the years, I was assigned to all three areas."

"Why did you stop working at the mill?"

"Got laid off. Over half a million people in the eighties struggled in that industry until the layoffs started. Someone told me that about 80% of the employees lost their jobs. I was somewhere near the beginning. Not the first to go, but not the last either."

"I take your point. It must have been tough. So how are you acquainted with the Moody family?"

"Who?"

"Stop acting stupid. Mark Moody, his wife, and two children. How do you know them?"

"I don't. I mean, I watch TV and listen to everything about them on the news. But I've never met them. I don't walk in their circles."

Landers stood and paced around the table, "Please explain why, on the night of the killings, witnesses saw your automobile parked in front of their residence."

"Are you sure it was mine? There are many similar cars around. If they are so sure, how come it took you so long to come to ask questions?" By this time, the suspect was struggling to control his stuttering.

"Cut the bullshit, Bobby. Why were you in the house? What did you witness?" Mansfield leaned forward, stopping mere inches from the older man's alcoholic nose. The tone of his voice became less friendly, and the temperature in the room changed.

"It was storming bad outdoors. I got scared when the thunder first roared and the lightning flashed. Although I still heard the rumbling, I felt safe inside but soon realized the sound came from upstairs, not outside."

"I counted three booms: one, followed by a short pause, and then another two. I hid in the kitchen when someone came down the stairs, entered the office, and left out the front door with what looked like a shotgun and a small bag." Due to the recording of the conversation, taking notes became unnecessary.

"How did you enter the house?"

"The back."

"Describe the person who went out the main entrance," Landers prodded.

"Average height, he wore drab clothes and had on a dark raincoat that came to his knees."

"Was he White, Black, Latino, or what?"

"No idea. He was just a shadow. I am quite sure he was male, but I don't have a reason for saying this." Bobby's croaky voice gave way to a husky, gravelly cough. He leaned forward, elbows sticking out like wings, his white forehead twisted in a ferocious old man's frown. He appeared fragile when compared to the two detectives.

Mansfield waited a full minute and asked, "What did you do after the man left?"

"Uh… Uh, I started to leave, but I wondered what happened upstairs. I thought someone might need some help."

"Go on. What did you find?"

"A lady was dead in the corridor on the second floor. Blood was everywhere. I turned to run away, missed the stairs, and ran into the doorpost of the next bedroom down the hallway. When I saw the two youngsters huddled together, I hauled it back to the stairway. Half of the girl's head was missing. I guess I panicked. I was sick on the steps but kept running outdoors to escape it all."

"Which door did you leave through?"

"The front. It was pouring down rain."

"All right," Mansfield said. "Let's take your story from the top. You are driving around one evening, and it starts thundering and lightning. You become scared, so you just happen to pull over at a random house, go to the back, break into the sliding doors, and overhear a triple homicide.”

“You remain hidden while the killer walks out of the front part of the house but cannot describe him. You ogle the bodies, run out, jump in your car, and drive away without notifying anyone. Does this sum it up?”

“Pretty much,” Bobby mumbled to no one in particular. He sat still, with his head hanging down and his hands folded. He did not look up at the men in front of him.

Chapter 38

Archer sat in silence for a long time. He filled the minutes with wonderment, pondering what might be taking the nice men so long. He was anxious to tell someone what was going on. With the arrival of the two detectives, he smiled broadly and welcomed them as house guests. A 'What's up with this geezer' look crossed between Mansfield and Landers.

"Hello, Mr. Cohen. We are the individuals assigned to the Moody murders. It looks like you experienced a hectic week."

"Yes, yes, I did. You folks can call me Archer. Everyone does."

"So, Archer, why did you and your pal decide to spend the night in the truck?" Mansfield began.

"We tried to avoid being seen by them. Sometimes they pretend to be the police or other authority figures. But we were lucky because you came with them. This way, we confirmed they were indeed law enforcement."

"What makes you think we are not policemen?"

"Because you are not wearing a uniform."

"I now understand. If not MPD, from whom are you trying to hide? Who is after you? Let us help," Mansfield asked, careful not to frighten the scared old man.

"I'm not sure who they are, but they are an organization or part of the government, and what they do is kidnap people and try to clone their DNA," Archer said quietly. "They can be anywhere, but at this point, I believe we have managed to escape." Mansfield glanced at Landers, agreeing that a wild trip was on the horizon.

"What exactly did you and Bobby do at the Angel Bluff house last Tuesday night?" Dave asked.

"I drove Bobby's car. We went to the house to steal documents, which would be the proof we needed to show these goons wanted to reproduce me."

"What is the connection between the house and cloning?" Landers asked, trying to keep calm but continuing to move things along.

"This is where they do all the planning. They decide whom to target, so you end up in a place resembling a hospital, but it isn't. They take your blood, give you pills, and put stuff in your I-V to make you sleep while they work on you, so you have no indication of what is happening. This is what they did to me before Bobby came and rescued me."

"All right, Archer, let's start at the beginning. How did you realize that the planning was done at the house?"

"Because Bobby said this was where we needed to go to steal the papers. I waited as the get-away driver."

"How long did you wait in the automobile?" Landers asked.

"Too long. It was harsh weather, thunder, lightning, and a horrible downpour. My friend took longer than he should have, so I got out of the car to check on him. When I got off the sidewalk, I got turned around because the heavy rain made it impossible to catch sight of the house, and someone came up and hit me on the head."

"The next thing, I woke up in one of their 'hospitals'. Once I was in that place, they kept asking questions and prying for information, but I didn't tell them a damned thing."

"How much time did you spend in this facility?" Mansfield asked.

"No idea. I stayed until one day when Bobby showed up and said we were going home, and we left. I told him all about it. He promised he would not leave until we were certain they had given up the hunt."

"Did he get the files you went to get?"

"Yes, but we were sidetracked when we heard dead bodies were in the house. I mentioned that I was aware it was a dangerous area. This is where they take the corpses of those who die during the cloning process. They take them to the house to dispose of them. That's why we hid all week: we have the documents, and now we hold their secrets."

"What do you mean you got sidetracked? Do you still possess the papers?" Landers asked, trying to hold back an exasperated attitude.

"Yes, when we remembered them, we opened the file, and nothing was there but blank pieces of paper. No plans, nothing was written, nothing at all. We went through all this danger and ended up with nothing. Now you understand why we did not come to you all. We had no proof."

"Wow, Archer, this is a fascinating account."

"You betcha. So the truth is it is all my fault that we went to Angel Bluff. It was me they wanted, not Bobby."

"How well are you acquainted with your friend? How long have you been besties?" Mansfield asked.

"Oh, we go back a good number of years. He used to work in the mills until he got laid off and became an entrepreneur. He was a businessman before losing his job but started doing it full-time after he left the factory. Without him, I'm not sure what I'd do."

"All right. Bobby is self-employed. Is this your description, or something he told you? What does an entrepreneur do?"

"That is how he describes himself. He does things for other people for a price. He says he wants to avoid getting into the inventory business, so he only performs for a fee. Everything is bound by a contract, which is both quite official and legal. He's a great capitalist."

"Can you describe his profession?" Landers pushed.

"No, I never cared much."

Chapter 39

While interviewing Archer, Mansfield ignored a call and let it go to voice mail. Once outside of the room, he picked up the message.

"Shit!" he exclaimed as he hung up the phone and turned to his partner. "TNT caught a case, and the victim had my card on his person. Guess who?" Landers looked at him and shrugged his shoulders. It might be the man on the moon after the interview he just ended.

"Luca Medina."

A small gasp followed his remark, "What the fuck, man?" With a quick bark of mad laughter, the detective added, "Why?"

"Hell, if anyone told me. I'm at the scene to look it over if you need me. Stay with these two. Return to Price and find out what business he is in and what he wants to steal from the Angel Bluff house. Also, try to talk Archer into volunteering a blood sample."

Mansfield stepped onto the crime scene, his eyes scanning the area for any signs of, he didn't really know, anything. The air carried a faint scent of decay and unease, mingling with the distant sounds of sirens and city nightlife.

Among the chaos, Mansfield's gaze fell on Max Thorn, towering above the crowd like a sentinel. Max's fiery red hair caught the light, creating an aura-like effect around his head. His broad frame projected a sense of strength and firmness, emphasized by his massive height of six-foot-four. Though his physical appearance hinted at a life filled with indulgence, his worn-out coat and frayed elbows told a tale of countless hours spent chasing down leads.

Max's face, from afar, seemed slender and angular, contrasting with his robust build. His complexion, pale as a Mexican tortilla, accentuated the vividness of his features. But it was his nose that commanded attention—a bulbous, crimson testament to the tolls of a life spent battling internal and external demons.

Max's expression shifted from focused intensity to a welcoming smile as Mansfield approached. He lifted his hand and gave a casual wave, displaying a sense of familiarity and camaraderie. Behind those seemingly carefree gestures, however, lay the unyielding determination and unwavering dedication that had earned him the nickname 'TNT'.

Max Thorn and Ellie Taylor formed a remarkable team—an explosion of energy and tenacity that refused to be deterred. They exemplified the spirit of 'Today-Not-Tomorrow', a mantra that echoed through their actions and choices. In the face of adversity, they remained resolute, unaffected by the shocks and surprises that came their way.

Ellie Taylor permitted Dave to enter the secured perimeter and walked him to the body. Even in uniform, she was attractive, with her long legs, toned arms, curly chestnut brown hair, and eyes that teased and smiled simultaneously. Dave lit a cigarette and put the burned match in his pocket. He crouched next to Medina like a baseball catcher.

The spike pounded into his heart caught his attention… which confirmed what he feared. He was to blame for Luca's death. Mansfield had tracked him down and made him valuable or potentially important; someone could not allow this.

The detective squatted by the body for a long while, taking in every tiny detail. Blood seeped out of the corners of the deceased mouth like red teardrops. With his elbows on his knees, holding a cigarette, he smoked and studied the body, making sure he wouldn't forget.

"So what do the techs have to offer?" Mansfield asked as he stood.

"Not a damned thing. If this is a gang hit, this is one of the cleanest in the books. No prints, no partials. Forensics says the stake is clean. No weapons, no wits," Thorn answered.

"You are aware this is not an organized thing," Dave looked at the two detectives, thinking they must be nuts.

"We do?" Taylor asked, dripping with sarcasm.

"Of course, gangs don't put stakes through people's hearts." Mansfield filled them in on the basics of the story behind Luca Medina, indicating he wasn't sure if he would end up being important to the triple homicide or not, but he had been on the suspect list.

"Who was aware you interviewed the kid, other than your partner?" Thorn asked.

"Well, the report is in the Murder Book, so anyone with access. We have not run down his alibi, so no one at his place of employment would be suspicious. However, one other person might be of interest, Jade Holmes. She is the coven leader from Buffalo and does not appear too enamored with Medina and his group. Hold on, here's her information." Mansfield took out his notebook and shared the notes from the interview. Taylor and Thorn jumped on the train with her as a suspect in a quick minute.

The next morning, Dave arrived at the station with two giant Starbucks. Swamped, Landers sat at his desk. Mansfield handed over one of the coffees to his partner.

"You look awful. Did you rest at all last night?"

"I slept in the back on one of the bunks. I had a change of clothes in the locker, so I'm fresh. You?"

"Made it home for a few hours of sleep and a shower. What did you find out from Price?"

"It's all about his profession. Archer was along for the journey when he went to the house on business. Bobby is a burglar-for-hire." Mansfield could not help himself and let out a full belly laugh.

"I'm not kidding. He gets contracts to burglarize places, bring out the goods, and turn them over to whoever is hiring him. Most of the time, he has no idea with whom he is negotiating. They arrange a time, place, and payment schedule. No questions asked. He receives some funds upfront and the remainder when the stolen items are delivered."

"The contract said to be at the Angel Bluff house at 10:30, but he arrived too soon. He wanted to finish before the rain started, so he went in early. He planned to pick up a file from the office on the first floor, so he didn't expect anyone to be home. Instead, while in the studio, he listened to the gunshots upstairs. He was on his way out when the murderer came down the stairs, and he hid in the kitchen. He said the person went into the office for a minute, then out the front door. The rest of his story stayed the same."

"Did the perp with the gun have the package before he went into the workroom or after?"

"He couldn't remember," Landers said, carefully sipping his steaming coffee.

"So what's all this with stealing DNA and cloning? Is his friend nuts or what?"

"Oh, that. Well, it turns out that as Bobby ran out the front, the rain was pouring down, and his visibility was nil. Consequently, he stumbled over Archer, who was lying in the yard. He had been hit and had a bad concussion, and Price took him to the hospital. They kept him overnight and released him the next afternoon. What we witnessed were the remnants of the injury. Bobby indicated the doctors said a few weeks might pass before his memory returned in full, if at all."

Both men sat for a few minutes, reflecting on the latest information and enjoying their coffee. At last, Mansfield spoke and filled Landers in on the Medina murder. He told Landers that signs of a struggle were present; however, the wooden stake through the heart was the ultimate cause of death.

"I sent Taylor and Thorn over to interview Jade Holmes. Can't wait to get wind on how that goes," Mansfield finished with a smirk.

"Assuredly, Medina is no longer a suspect. What are your thoughts regarding Price?" Landers asked.

"He ended up being at the wrong house at an inopportune hour. He was supposed to be the murderers' scapegoat, but he botched the job. We went through both of their homes and found no guns, ammo, or other evidence of a violent nature. Let's keep him without charging him until we have to let him go. Did you obtain a blood sample from Cohen?"

"No problem. He was happy to give it," Landers answered.

"Good. Let's transport the specimen over to Sol so that he can match it to the shotgun butt. Let's go ahead and kick the older man for now. I doubt he's going anywhere. Now we concentrate on Jake Mendoza, the Miami Gun Club, and Charles Gray although he has an alibi."

Chapter 40

Mansfield reflected on the situation at Freedom Pointe, and a disquieting absence lingered. The taste of worry crept on his tongue, a bitter flavor that made his stomach churn. The silence surrounding him was deafening, like a heavy blanket muffling all sounds. This void could be a sign, he thought. The absence of contact might suggest that all was well, that his mother was simply enjoying her days without any need for concern.

Instead, he dialed Peter Ekker's number. As the phone rang, the sound reverberated throughout the virtual room, a familiar melody that hinted at the connection to a trusted friend. Ekker's voice greeted him at the other end.

In their conversation, Peter's words painted a vivid picture. Dave could almost taste the atmosphere of the antique shop, a blend of aged wood, dust, and the faint scent of nostalgia. He pictured Thomas Blair shutting down the shop for the holidays, the excitement evaporating like the last whiff of a fading perfume.

Peter's voice grew animated as he described Blair's intentions. Mansfield could hear the flicker of anticipation in his tone as if he could taste the adventure ahead. The idea of a buying trip, a journey to far-off lands, filled the conversation with an exotic aroma, like the spices of foreign cuisines carried on a distant breeze.

However, during the excitement, a sudden shift occurred. The mention of the DEA brought a metallic tang to the air, a taste of danger and intrigue. Mansfield's heart skipped a beat as Peter revealed that Thomas had been tracked to South America. The image of bustling streets and the harshness of voices flooded Dave's mind, accompanied by the vibrant colors and lively scents of a pulsating marketplace. Then, like a mirage vanishing into thin air, Thomas disappeared among the multitudes, blending in effortlessly, leaving the DEA lost and bewildered.

When Dave inquired about Thomas' mother, Peter indicated that no activity had been reported since the burglary attempt. The local cops still drove by, and Bee had been shown how to operate her monitoring system device, which she was instructed to wear constantly. Because Jackie also wore one, Dave understood what he was talking about perfectly.

"I hate to ask, but did you find anything on this Caspar fellow?"

"Your instincts were right on this one. He was last spotted departing the retirement complex in a dark sedan on the morning of the attack on Ms. Blair, and he hasn't been seen since. In addition to leaving behind all his stuff, the administration reported him as missing. Of course, once the police checked the information he provided on his application, it became evident that everything was fraudulent."

"He wasn't missing; he had taken off. His entire existence at the Pointe amounted to nothing but deception. I'm sure his presence dealt with finding the antiquities and Blair." After thanking Peter, the detective hung up and considered calling Jackie. Without much thought, he contacted Slater instead.

"Hey, Rita. This is Dave. I'm heading down to Coconut Grove to pick up a person of interest in the Angel Bluff case. Care to meet me as backup? This guy has anger issues and might become a little riled."

"Where's Landers?"

"He's picking up the second suspect. We're down to one of two guys, but I don't want word to circulate to either of them, so we are scooping them up separately."

"Where, when?" Slater asked.

"Noon. He is supposed to be at the Bizcaya Grill. His receptionist says there are no customers, so I think he's having a liquid lunch."

"I wouldn't miss this for the world. Check your radio in case something comes up."

Dave hung up and smiled to himself. There was something about that woman he liked. Something comfortable. The paperwork came through, and Mansfield and Landers charged out the back door like it was the War of 1812. Landers jumped onto the MacArthur Causeway East and headed to the island. Once there, he took a right on Alton Road. The Miami Beach Police were at the Yacht Club waiting for him. Bringing Charles Gray in happened without incident, and he waited in the holding area.

Dave took US 1 South to Coconut Grove, pulling into the parking lot of the Grill seconds before Slater's squad car. She and her partner got out and accompanied him into the establishment. Once they showed their IDs to the host, they found the person they were looking for sitting on a stool at the elaborate, well-stocked bar. The backup stood to the side as Mansfield approached him to announce himself.

"Jake Mendoza, Dave Mans…" was all he got out of this mouth.

Mendoza looked at the mirrored back bar and spotted the investigator. Jake's back muscles tightened, and Mansfield looked in the mirror and noted Jake's teeth were clenched, and he had a sudden twitch like a madman. Having grabbed the Corona bottle by the neck with his right hand, Mendoza stood and spun counterclockwise toward his left shoulder to catch the detective off guard. In less than a second, Mansfield stepped back half a step and leaned the upper portion of his body back further, allowing the weapon to miss his head by several inches.

Angrier because of the miss, Mendoza now brought the bottle back in a backhanded swing toward Mansfield's head. Following his training, Dave moved in, closed the distance, and blocked the return strike with both forearms. The glass container crashed to the ground. The detective grabbed Mendoza's wrists and snapped his elbow over his forearm. At this point, the scrap was over. Mansfield pushed Mendoza over the bar stool and completed saying what he had to say.

Slater stood with her mouth catching flies. All of this happened in seconds, but she still couldn't get it straight in her mind. Mansfield marched the now calm suspect over to her and asked if she would take him for medical treatment and, afterward, take him to a holding cell downtown.

Rita looked at Mansfield and said, "Wha… What just happened here?"

"Returning the Storm," Mansfield replied as he left the establishment.

Rita and her partner took Mendoza to the emergency room to fix the elbow. While waiting for the X-rays, she put in a call to Landers.

"Where are you?" Slater asked.

"In the squad room, wondering why you all are taking so long. Why? You sound like you are about to jump out of your skin. What's up?"

"I'm at Mercy Hospital."

"What the hell, are you injured? Dave, is he hurt?" Landers jumped to his feet and started walking toward the door.

"Nope. Everything is fine. We are good. Mendoza is the one with the problem. Mansfield beat the shit out of him, but it was so quick. I mean seconds, a blur, and I must have missed something."

"All right," Landers said, exhaling as he returned to his desk. "Take a breath and tell me what happened."

"The suspect was on a bar stool. Dave walked up, began to announce, and he turned and attempted to hit him with a beer bottle."

Landers let out a hefty laugh. "Well, that was his first mistake."

"No kidding. He missed and tried again but ended up with a broken elbow. I have never seen anyone move so fast in my life."

"What did Dave say?"

"Something about a storm and for me to take Mendoza to medical and nothing stronger than Tylenol for pain. Then downtown to a holding cell. Then he left."

Again, Landers laughed. "It's all good, Rita. He was on the boxing team in college for six years. When he came to Miami, he found karate. For 10 years, he competed in tournaments, traveling worldwide. He's a third-degree black belt."

"Are you kidding me? I never would have guessed. It sure isn't public knowledge. You would never know by being around him or talking with him," Rita said with caution.

"That's the whole point. When you have the skills, you don't need to use them under normal conditions. Damn, I wish I had been with you. I have only seen him in action once or twice or at exhibition events when he's only playing around."

"Boy, I am much better after talking to you. No idea where he went, but I should be there in a couple of hours."

Landers grinned as he hung up. It wasn't but a few minutes before he received a call from his partner. He sat back in his chair, considering what the topic of the conversation would be. On the third ring, he finally answered.

"I understand you ran into some action getting your guy."

"You might say that. Rita's cleaning up my mess. But that's not why I called. I'm on my way to the station and should arrive in about 10 minutes. Thought we could get a jump on Gray if you were back."

"I'm here and waiting."

"Great. Before we go in, have you received any news on the shotgun from the boys in Doral yet?"

"Sure did. I was waiting for you to get here. It was a match. That's our weapon for all three murders. Also, the blood on the butt matches Archer Cohen."

"Oh man, this is what I wanted to hear."

Chapter 41

As Charles Gray was escorted into the small interview room, the metallic click of the door closing behind him echoed in the confined space, sending a shiver down his spine. The room seemed to close in on him, the air thick with anticipation. He sat at the table, his palms damp with sweat and his gaze consumed by the empty chairs opposite him.

Restlessness began to grip Gray, manifesting in the rhythmic tapping of the last three fingers of his right hand against the tabletop. The sound vibrated through the room, a nervous beat echoing in his ears. The tangible sensation of his fingers meeting the hard surface provided a brief distraction from the growing tension that filled the air.

As minutes turned into an endless period, Gray's unease grew. The silence crowded in on him, an uncomfortable weight that threatened to suffocate his thoughts. He shifted in his seat, feeling the unpleasant scrape of the chair against the linoleum floor. The creaking sound deepened the sense of confinement, increasing his growing anxiety.

His eyes darted around the room and landed on the one-way glass, a transparent barrier separating him from the outside world. Through it, Gray was sure he saw two detectives, their expressions unreadable, observing his every move. The knowledge of their scrutiny only heightened his nervousness, like a spotlight on his every flaw.

Gray began to pace back and forth, rehearsing his responses to the questions he anticipated would come his way. The taste of expectation mingled with the metallic tang of anxiety in his mouth, creating a bitter cocktail of emotions. The waiting game continued.

Within the ranks of the MPD, Mansfield was regarded as a masterful interrogator, a reputation earned through years of honing his craft. He possessed an innate ability to navigate the complex maze of human psychology, smoothly extracting truths from the shadows of deceit. His approach was methodical and strategic, comparable to an artist systematically painting a suspect into a corner.

Mansfield's interrogation tactics were designed to evoke a sense of unease, to unravel the composure of even the most hardened individuals. He used his words precisely, asking probing questions and observing keenly as the suspect's façade cracked under mounting fear. He knew that silence held power, so he would often step back, allowing the deafening quiet to fill the room, watching as the discomfort grew and confession seemed the only escape.

Nevertheless, Dave's skills were not fueled by personal gain or a thirst for dominance. His expertise was merely a part of his professional responsibilities. The art of extracting the truth, the ability to elicit confessions, was woven into the very fabric of his job.

"Well, let's get at it," the interrogator said, and he and his partner entered the small room.

"I would shake your hand, but I don't think so. Forgive my rudeness," the pretentious man standing next to the wooden chair said.

"Stop the bullshit," Mansfield retorted. "I'm in no mood to play your games. Your boyfriend is nowhere around to be impressed, so let's cut the nonsense. Who are you, and what country are you from?"

"We covered this. I am Charles…"

Landers knocked the suspect's chair over on its side. He flew, hitting his head on the floor and sliding until he landed against the wall. The younger detective walked over without emotion, lending a hand, making it easier for the man to reach his feet.

"Wow, you need to be more careful, Mr. Gray. Stop moving around so much. The floors here can be slippery," Landers commented as he put the chair upright and helped him back to the table.

"I ask again since you give the impression of someone ready to respond: who are you, and where do you come from?" Mansfield repeated.

"I don't understand the question."

"Listen," the detective started, controlled and direct, "Your paper trail is useless. None of the information you gave us was true. Your social security number is stolen, your passport is fake, the works, and all done with expertise. You have an accent that is Eastern European, Slovak, I'm sure. English is not your native language."

"The entire story about the Shinnecock is crap. Furthermore, your swamp name is Romanian, which means Dark Soul. Looking at the records, you arrived in the USA in 1987, around 18 years old, under the name Charles Gray. I want to understand where you lived for the first 18 years of your life."

The pompous man deflated like a dog's toy. He looked like Charles, with black skin and full lips, but his palms covered his eyes, his shoulders slumped, and he resembled a failed soldier. For a long time, he said nothing. He remained as still as a stone and barely breathed. At last, breaking his silence, he spoke like he was in a trance or a dream.

"The caves. I stayed in the caves," Charles started. He dropped his hands and looked at the detectives with strange eyes. For the first time, Dave became aware that his eyes were a clear, pale brown, like amber from the tall forests on the west coast. But now, there was a disturbing quality to them. His determination had left him. A peculiar weight wrapped around his limbs as he gave up.

"What caves?" Mansfield asked, pausing between each question.

"In Romania. I lived beyond expectations and escaped. No one cared. One less mouth to feed, I guess. I wanted to join the family on the hill when I was younger, but they did not want me. After an accident at their house where some kids died, I ran. Some revolutionaries found me and took me to the underground chambers under the large, strong buildings built on top of the mountain with high rock walls. They hid me from the authorities."

"How young?"

"I don't know; I think over 10."

"Are you referring to a castle?"

"Yes. The place where the leader of the vampires lives. Over here, you all call it Dracula's Castle, but this isn't the real name. We only moved around during the day and remained hidden at night. The people against communist rule educated me on how to read and write, and they taught me English. For many years, I helped in the kitchen to pay my way to being part of the organization."

"One night, some years later, Dragos came to me with papers and explained that I was leaving for the USA. I needed to forget everything in Romania. I had a new name and everything, but they sent me to a related place in New York to stay until I got settled. He and a few others took me from the caves, and the next thing I remember, people escorted me to Buffalo. My papers said I was 18. The only name I answered to before I came to the United States was Suflet Intunecat because that is what they called me before I escaped from the orphanage.”

“What was waiting for you in the Queen City?”

“If I talk about it, I’m dead. It is a place where I stayed until I earned my freedom. You earn your release in many ways in a place like that.” When he tried to laugh, he only made a scary cackle because he was under so much stress that his vocal cords had tightened. The detectives witnessed the trembling in his thighs as he discussed this subject.

“Were you a Black Swan?” Landers asked. This query would begin the flow of sweat down the man’s spine if he weren’t perspiring at present.

By the time he finished answering, Charles had moist eyes and pupils that appeared flecked with gold, like pebbles. Mansfield looked across the table at the man. He was dreadful, and yet, the most alluring, tortured soul he had ever met.

“Why did you tell us you did not own any guns? It was so easy to check. You have two registered,” Landers wondered.

“I was afraid having firearms was bad. I keep them at the gun club, so they are not near me. I just like shooting for sport, and I like to find out who can do it better. Maybe I should have been honest.”

“How about the shotgun at the firehouse?” Mansfield asked. “That one is not registered.”

“It is not mine.”

“So why do you have it?”

“An associate asked me to hold on to it for him.”

“What friend? Someone from the club? What is his name?” Landers demanded.

“Yes, Jake Mendoza.”

“Charles, we have people there now, going through your things looking for ammunition that goes with the gun. They are also looking through your house for the same thing. You know that you are in big trouble if they find any. Are you sure you want to stick with this story?” the investigator challenged.

“Yes. It is the truth.”

Mansfield and Landers left the room. The search warrants for Gray and Mendoza’s lockers at the club and their homes had been authorized to seek the ammunition and the steins earlier that day. Landers ensured teams executed those documents immediately after the suspects were in custody.

Mansfield went to the break room and got a Pepsi. He glanced over at the snack machine and wanted the juicy fruit gum. His mouth watered in anticipation, but he remembered. He was unsure if the stitches were still present, but the hole in his gum appeared to be healing, and that process was not to be jeopardized. Instead, he opted to walk away.

Chapter 42

Back at his desk, he spotted Slater talking to Landers. He went over to find out Mendoza's medical status. Even though his broken elbow had been repaired, the man's spirit remained damaged. Rita put him in room #5. While Mike left word to be notified when anything came back on the search warrants, Dave ordered a large pizza for delivery to the interview room.

"Well, Jake, the journey matters. So we need to talk about your roaming and how you ended up sitting here, in this interrogation space, in front of me and Landers over here," Mansfield began as he nodded at his partner.

"Let's start with your alibi. You said you entertained customers trying to close a deal on the evening of October 19 and that you would give us your itinerary and the names of the customers. But not a peep from you since we visited your office. Now, you must understand how this looks. Your evasiveness causes you to look guilty. Do you care to share information now?"

"I was with the McCall Group president, Bryce Hatcher, the CFO, Ruben Patel, and their strategic acquisitions guy, Andrew Turner. They are looking for some real estate to build a new corporate headquarters. We ate at The Black Tulip Restaurant, where we had reservations for four at six. After dinner, we went to the Capricious Panthers for some T&A. I got home a little after 11:00." Landers left at once to verify the information and check the credit card charges. The house security company's log data confirmed his arrival time at the residence.

"That did not seem so bad. Let's hope you are telling the truth. Was your wife home when you arrived?"

"Yes."

"Last time we talked, you said you didn't have a relationship with anyone named Charles Gray. Do you want to amend this statement?"

"Since you mentioned it, I looked him up in the register at the gun club, and I do recognize this person. I didn't put the face and name together. He's

Mark Moody's companion; thus, I usually think of him when discussing my friend. I apologize for my misrepresentation."

"Good, glad we got that cleared up. Mr. Gray visited for a long talk and said he didn't own a shotgun, even though we found one in his room in the fire station closet. He was not forthcoming. Have you ever seen him with a pump action at the club?"

"No."

"You indicated you do not own this type of firearm, and one is not registered to you. However, in the end, Charles gave you up and told us you gave him the weapon and asked him to hold on to it for you. He couldn't take it home because Mark doesn't like weapons in the house, so he took it to the station."

"I have no way of predicting why he would say that. I never asked him to do such a thing," Jake answered incredulously.

A slight knock at the door sounded, and Mansfield turned and motioned for the knocker to come in. The front desk officer delivered a pizza, along with sodas and napkins. It was an enticing perfume that most people around the world would recognize. The alluring fragrance of melting mozzarella cheese, sauce, pepperonis, jalapenos, and sausage filled the small space with a pizzeria-like aroma, and the two men gorged themselves. Mansfield cleaned up the remnants and took the remaining slices outside the cell-like area.

Landers confirmed the reservations at The Black Tulip. He now waited for a call to confirm the time and the charges with the Capricious Panthers. The searches at the gun club yielded no results. The same thing happened when Charles Gray's house was searched. MPD headed to Jake Mendoza's address last. They saved it for the end, waiting for Lee Mendoza to arrive home, so they could enter without damaging the property. Mansfield told him to return to the interview after he had answers.

"If I recall, when we visited you at your office, there were quite a few trophies indicating your love of hunting. Didn't you tell us you learned to hunt from your father?"

"I probably did. I don't recall. But that is accurate," Mendoza said, wondering where the detective was going.

"So where is your dad nowadays?"

"He passed several years ago."

"I'm sorry. Whatever happened to his shotgun? The one in the picture you mentioned was your father's. It looked like a Winchester pump 12-gauge."

Jake sat there, staring at Mansfield. All he needed to do to keep from storming over the table and exacting his revenge was to think about the agonizing pain shooting through his forearm. He convinced himself that the Tylenol the doctor gave him slowed his reflexes, and his mind had the sensation of wading through the subtropical wilderness of the Everglades. One misstep, and he would be gator bate.

"Jake, are your ears working? Where did your father's shotgun go after he died?" the interrogator asked again.

"I inherited the cabin and all his belongings," he replied. Might as well tell the truth. It was too easy to verify.

"And…"

"Everything is still mine."

"So you do have ownership of the shotgun," Mansfield repeated.

"According to the facts, yes, but I don't think of it as belonging to me. It's Dad's gun," Jake tried to explain his way out of the lie he had been caught in.

Landers entered the interview room and took a seat. He looked over at his partner with a smile on his face. "So, Mendoza, guess what we've been working on? Forget I asked. We executed a search warrant on your residence and found slugs for the weapon used in the murder of the Moody's. Now, what are you doing with this ammunition at your house if you don't own a shotgun?" Landers boasted.

"Jake, this isn't playing too well for you. Your inherited gun is a 12-gauge; the firearm shells are in your house; a witness says you asked him to hold this weapon for you, and it is the one used to shoot three people. What is a detective to think?" Mansfield asked.

"Must be a coincidence. I'm telling you, I was out with customers when all this occurred."

"Well, my man," Landers added, "the icing is that the three antique steins missing from the Angel Bluff house were also in a closet at your house. What happened that caused this?"

Jake's stare bore into the detective's soul, its intensity etching the officer's name in stone. The weight of realization settled on him like a suffocating fog as whispers in his mind grew louder, forging clarity among the haze of confusion. Lee's timing suddenly revealed a disturbing motive—the discussions about parting ways had only surfaced once she discovered Evie's impending divorce. But the true revelation struck Jake when he disclosed that Evie planned to relocate to Europe, an invitation seemingly excluding Lee.

Visions flickered in Jake's mind, replaying the moments he paraded around the house, intoxicated with jubilation. He could almost hear his tuneless humming, the chant of 'The wicked witch is leaving', permeating the air as he relished the anticipation of newfound wealth. He focused solely on himself, oblivious to Lee's emotional state. How had she genuinely felt during that time? He strained to summon those memories, to remember the depth of her devastation—did he miss this?

Returning home from the Capricious Panthers, his heart clenched with anguish when he discovered Lee perched on the front steps, her body swaying and her grip on the shotgun desperate and unwavering. At that moment, he believed she had attempted to end her life and had faltered in her tragic endeavor. Oh, how mistaken he had been.

Since the killings stained their lives, any talk of divorce had fallen silent, swallowed by the chilling void left in the wake of the murders. Had Lee been absent from their home on that horrible night? Jake's mind raced, plagued by the lingering doubt of whether he had set this catastrophic chain of events into motion. As fragments of conscious thought gradually connected, time unraveled the deception, revealing an intricate web of clues that threatened to expose an unthinkable truth.

Mansfield intended to wait Jake out while he processed. Without warning, he jumped up and motioned for his partner to follow. In the hallway, he told Landers to put an APB on Lee Mendoza and immediately send someone back to her house to catch her before she bolted.

"It was the wife, Landers. It was her, not him. As he assembled the pieces, his expression shifted in a big way. I don't understand all that happened, but Jake was unaware of those steins."

"How can that be? The data from the security company put her in the house before the shootings," Mike argued.

"Does it? Think hard. Does the information indicate when she logs in and out of the house, or do they merely note when her code number is used? What if she left the house at 9:30?"

"Oh, shit."

Chapter 43

While waiting to find out if they picked up Lee Mendoza, Mansfield called Nora Randolph, the district attorney, and filled her in on the situation with Charles Gray. This guy's paperwork was bullshit, but he was no longer a suspect in the homicide case. He would be needed to testify at trial. If it meant anything, during the investigation, Landers found he had lived a clean life and paid taxes every year since he arrived in the USA. But Randolph had the option of reporting him to immigration and sending him back to Romania. The DA said she would call the detective back.

Mansfield also shared that they had Robert Price in custody. He told her about the events and his belief that the man had been set up. However, despite having intended to break into the residence, all he took appeared to be a few blank sheets of paper, which was impossible to establish. Instead, he ended up being an unwilling witness to a triple homicide. His presence at the house had been proven via DNA evidence, but he was not the shooter. Nora said to kick him. Nothing interested her.

"She's outta here," Landers exclaimed, breaking the silence in the room.

"Damn. We're too late. I bet she bolted the minute the search team left," his partner replied. He stood and walked down the hall to the interview room, anger making his strides stiff and jerky. Landers jumped up and followed.

Bursting into room #5, Mansfield shouted, "Your future depends on your answer to my next question. You can be charged as an accessory to three murders or as the perpetrator of murder on three counts. It's up to you. Question: Where is your wife? Bullshit answers count, so think before you speak." Jake sat and stared at the detectives, from one to the other, hoping for some assistance from Landers.

Landers responded to the silent plea for help, "I'm smiling… That alone should scare you."

Mendoza appeared pitiful. His sling gave the impression of having been placed on him by an adversary, and it looked to be suffocating. His chin was dark blue and black to match his swollen arm. Silence filled the room as he thought hard about what he would say. He opened his mouth; nothing came out; and he closed it immediately. None of his lines of usual bullshit would help him out of this situation.

He considered his wife, which was not something Jake often did. A sense of guilt must be weighing on her. He understood her anger at Evie, but *why would she kill the children?* She loved kids; at least, he thought she did. He thought this was what she talked about all the time. School and the little people. Never her family, never much of anything else, except, of course, divorcing her husband. But he had been wrong about everything else.

"I think she would be riddled with guilt, so I doubt she would flee the area. My hunch is that she went to one of two locations. Either back to the Moody's or back to the school," Jake answered, realizing his world had been torn apart.

Without saying a word, both detectives exited the interview room. Landers took the place of employment, and Mansfield took the residence. Landers arrived at the establishment first to find it fully locked up. As the security guard returned from his rounds, he found the premises empty. No cars were in the parking areas, and Lee Mendoza did not appear near the grounds.

Dave arrived at the Angel Bluff house, observing its untouched external face. Lee's car was conspicuously absent. Exiting his vehicle, he approached the front door, ensuring it remained securely locked. To his astonishment, the door yielded to his touch, swinging open. Stepping inside, he called out Lee's name, but his voice was met with an eerie stillness. Gripping his Glock tightly, he meticulously searched the untouched lower level, finding no signs of disturbance.

Ascending the stairs, Dave's footsteps echoed in the house's silence. He veered to the right, clearing the primary bedroom. Continuing down the hall, his back pressed against the wall; he cautiously advanced toward the children's rooms. Before crossing the threshold of Cooper's room, he halted, straining his ears for any hint of sound. Silence persisted.

Employing the slicing the pie technique, Mansfield hastened his pace, minimizing his exposure in the danger zone without overlooking crucial details. His firearm remained trained on his visual focus as he moved diagonally toward the corner of the room. His sharp eyes scanned the surroundings in a sweeping motion, momentarily halting when a shape on Cooper's bed registered. Angling himself for a clear view of the object, he recognized it as a woman clasping a toy belonging to the child. Urgently, he called out to her and received no response. He identified himself as a law enforcement officer and repeated his command, only to be met with an unsettling silence that hung in the air.

The detective went over to the body and checked for a pulse, which was slight and irregular. Looking into this woman's face, he recognized her as the suspect. He also noted the empty bottle of pills lying on the bed beside her. He radioed for help and backup right away.

The ambulance took Lee Mendoza to the hospital. She died on the way without saying a word. Landers notified Jake of her death since he was her next of kin. Mansfield called Nora and explained the situation. Jake's alibi had checked out, so he didn't commit the murders. She said to arrest him as an accessory after the fact and book him.

When Mansfield's phone rang after a long, exhausting day, he answered it with a yawn. It was Detective Thorn.

"Hey, Dave. Thanks for the intel on this Jade Holmes character."

"What do you mean? I thought you might enjoy a little of that sassy attitude."

"Let me tell you what she said to me," Max said, with an unbridled note of excitement in his voice. "She told me to shut up! That she wears heels bigger than my dick." They both rolled with laughter.

"I want to marry that bitch."